CW01497710

Teach Her

Mark Kotting

Legend Press Ltd, The Old Fire Station, 140 Tabernacle Street, London, EC2A 4SD

info@legend-paperbooks.co.uk | www.legendpress.co.uk

Contents © Mark Kotting 2014
The right of the above author to be identified as the author of this work has been asserted in accordance with the Copyright, Designs and Patent Act 1988. British Library Cataloguing in Publication Data available.

Print ISBN 978-1-9098785-7-0
Ebook ISBN 978-1-9098785-8-7

Set in Times
Cover design by Gudrun Jobst www.yotedesign.com
Printed in the United Kingdom by TJ International.

All rights reserved. No part of this publication may be reproduced, stored in or introduced into a retrieval system, or transmitted, in any form, or by any means electronic, mechanical, photocopying, recording or otherwise, without the prior permission of the publisher. Any person who commits any unauthorised act in relation to this publication may be liable to criminal prosecution and civil claims for damages.

Legend 🕮 Press
Independent Book Publisher

Mark Kotting is from London. He has written TV and radio comedy including two plays for BBC Radio, 'The Match' and 'Gulf'.

Mark also is the author of *Nappy Rash* and *Babble and Squeak*.

To everyone who has helped me.

To T,
for watching over me.

Chapter 1

Shirley knew it was coming to an end.

Of course she did, she was ending it. Shirley knew because she got paid to know, was good at knowing, she'd won awards for knowing. She knew things as a girl, knew things as a wife, as a teacher.

What she didn't know, under her French bob, her blue eyes, her five foot five frame, was how her only child would feel when he returned to the break, the split, the lancing, the end of his parent's marriage. She didn't know that.

She hoped he'd choose to live with her, she wasn't sure. He loved his dad. Jim wasn't a bad man, wasn't boring. It was just that their relationship, their love had turned cold, like a slice of uneaten beef on a Sunday plate, might as well throw on the cold gravy.

Shirley had sorted out a flat, a new home for a new life. The agent had shown her everything on his books. He'd have shown his own grandmother's grave if he'd thought he'd get money for sleeping on it. He'd never left his home town and was in debt due to the double-barrelled exhaust on his car and the tattoos over his arms, Sanskrit on one, Chinese on the other, couldn't remember if it was Cantonese or Mandarin. Couldn't remember what the writing meant, nothing mattered but selling space and the scent of money.

For a young man who hadn't gone far, his arms had, they'd been around the world. He was saving for another on his neck, didn't know if it was going to be a butterfly or a bat. He'd never know when to stop, he was the same with conversation.

Shirley studied his arms. All those young wasted minds, not using the education put in front of them, not gobbling it up. She'd come to the conclusion that their time, the time of the Western youth, was nearly up. The Asian tsunami was heading their way and she didn't mean a wave or quake. No, she meant Chinese followed by Indians, with gyrating Brazilians behind and their desire to learn and move on up. Shirley imagined a time when Europe would be a massive theme park. That was it, no other work would exist: Europe's population standing around in costumes, emptying milk churns, Morris dancing around a pole as hordes of marauding tourists disembark from coaches, following tour leaders holding flags, so no-one gets lost. Education, what's a child without an education? Nothing more than an adult hiding their nappy, swaddled in their own ignorance, she'd always thought.

Shirley had twenty-eight years of a teacher's pension saved up, a finishing line in sight and a little juice still left in her instructor's tank to limp there.

She knew all this, but what she hadn't known was just how sad she would feel, she wipes a tear from her cheek. Then another, they'd started to flow. If she'd known this, would she have stuck the ring to the card? Yes. It was them, him and her and what they'd become, the bickering, the point scoring.

She'd left him in bed, listening to the radio as she did most mornings, bent over and whispered have a nice day, meant it. She didn't wish him harm, wasn't after revenge, just wanted away.

It was cold outside. What did anyone expect? It was the New Year for Christ's sake, the same month as Jim's surname and the sun wouldn't be peeping for another hour, wouldn't be warming for months.

Of all the months to be called, I go and get married to a January.

Shirley had shouted once, after one of their first arguments.

Could have been worse, love, could have been Shirley May.

Jim June would have been worse, or April or March. He'd been through all the months and he was more than happy to be a January. Reckons he got the best surname out of the lot.

Jim June?

Jim March?

Jim April?

Jim February?

No, Jim was more than happy being a January. Jim January sounded like someone who might have lived in cowboy times or at least ridden a horse. He'd done neither.

He pushes himself from his bed, pulls the roman blind. He's never got the hang of it, so they stick half way up. Something about pulling the cords at the same tension, he'd been told, still he couldn't do it. More to the point couldn't be bothered. Shirley hates the look of the house when he leaves them like this, reckons it looks like a junk on the seas.

Jim turns, walks downstairs in his pyjamas, the drawstring has gone. He'd asked Shirley to fix them when she had the sewing machine out, she hadn't, so he uses one hand to hold them up as he moves along. There's a card on the table, a card with a ring stuck to it, his ring, his card.

He hadn't bought much in life, but he'd definitely bought that. He hadn't skimped, the jeweller who'd sold it said that it would be a solid investment, that he couldn't go wrong.

It wasn't looking that way now. He'd heard that all the gold ever dug up would only fill an ordinary size semi and here he was looking at his little bit. And what had he heard on the radio just this very morning. In his slumber as he drifted in and out, heard Shirley's feet, the zip on the skirt. What had he heard? That the world's most expensive tuna ever had just been hauled in over the side and sold for seven hundred thousand dollars. A bloody fish. Made him want to get up and buy a rod.

He looks at the card, it says:

I can't be this person anymore.

He recognises the writing, knows the ring, knows the finger it should be on. Jim couldn't call the way he and Shirley communicated now as talking. More lulls before reloads. The end of their marriage had crept up on them like a bush fire and burnt them out.

They couldn't help themselves. They'd neither the patience nor the desire to listen to what was being said by the other. They hadn't heard the end of each other's sentences in years. They assumed they knew what was to come. Assumed they'd heard it all before. The patience well, the tap had dried up.

Hence the card. Hence the departure. Hence no longer having a wife. Well, she's finally gone and done it. He couldn't say there hadn't been plenty of warning shots, he sighs and shakes his head.

Chapter 2

Shirley was on her second cup of coffee by the time her husband picked up the card. She'd already been too hasty taking off a pair of gloves and tying up a young boy's laces, a tug here and a pull there, everyday stuff, she'd done it a thousand times before. Today, though, she was struggling, really struggling. She'd noticed that she'd pulled them a little harder, tighter, more firmly than she'd have normally done, more distracted. She'd taken out her frustrations on a helpless child. And when another had shown her a picture, beaming at his crayon delight, Shirley hadn't smiled back, hadn't really looked or given the praise he was so desperate to hear.

I'm sorry, Ben.

She said, catching herself, correcting herself. She knew others who didn't smile at the children. Like a marriage, there was nothing worse than a jaded teacher. A teacher who didn't care, a teacher who'd had enough, a teacher who wouldn't go that extra yard. She knew of at least three of her ducklings (that's what she called her special ones) who had gone on to Oxford. It made her proud, proud that all her hours of teaching, the funnelling of information had paid off. She'd received a thank you card from one of them, saying that she'd owed it to her, Miss Petticoat. Her first teacher at school who'd opened the gate of education. She loved that card, had it framed, it made all the hours and years, worth it. Children down here didn't often end up in educational Meccas like that. No, they waited passively for whatever life would bring.

Miss Petticoat walks away from the small tables, the small people, the noise and takes herself to the toilet. She locks the door and puts her head to it, starts to cry. Hadn't cried like this in years.

What have I done? What have I done?

She repeats, like a chant.

All her confidence is leaving. All the whys no longer make sense. She can't talk about it with her classroom assistant, who is half her age and irritating. They had nothing in common, just chitter chatter and lesson plans. The only thing she can really remember with any certainty coming out of the young woman's mouth was that she'd married some guitarist from a small selling band that had made the national papers. That he'd serenaded her at the foot of the bed on her marriage night. That she'd fallen asleep in her white wedding dress as he played on and on. He was still playing when she woke up. She'd laughed after she'd told her story. Shirley hadn't found it funny, hadn't found it funny at all. She'd wanted to say:

You fool, he's more in love with his guitar than he'll ever be with you.

No, Shirley wasn't going to talk privately, candidly to her, what would have been the point? No, she'd rather take her chances in the toilet behind a closed door with children on the other side waiting to be educated.

Jim was once a romantic. Was, before the rust set in. He'd been so excited on the day Shirley had said yes. He'd given her time to consider, reconsider. Nothing beat that day, the day the ring had been slipped onto her outstretched finger, to show the world she was his, that tiny ring and all it stood for. And here it was now, stuck to a card with his wife's fingerprint showing forensically on the tape.

Is this the start of my graveyard song? He thinks. It happens, wives leaving husbands, Jim hears about it, sees it in other men, the lack of care, the ill health, the decline. He picks up the card, on one side the ring, the other a picture of a man pulling a donkey. It looks slightly Greek, wearing a hat, long ears poking through. He doesn't have the heart to pull the ring. Drops the whole lot, the ring, the Greek donkey in his pocket and looks out of the window. It's not everyday Jim wakes up to this. He realises he's crying, tears dropping from head height to gloss.

Outside it's snowing, it surprises him. His marriage had gone from confetti to snow. Walking in it is a young man, a bloated dad, driving his child in a remote controlled car. His kid, his protégé, his young-un, his spunk, his sperm is slumped at the wheel. Jim can't tell if the baby is awake or not. The car swamps him as the card has done to Jim. The dad keeps driving with his head bent against the snow, drives his sleeping, slumped bundle of joy into a wall, spilling the child head first onto the pavement.

Jim moves closer to the window for inspection, watches the lumbering dad pick up his distraught doomed child (Jim's heard too many stories about these kids from Shirley to think anything different). The father bends, he still has one hand in his pocket. He couldn't make the job any harder. Bored and disinterested he flips the car with his foot. Drops the kid, his spunk, his sperm, his pride back in and says, Jim can hear, it's shouted more than said:

It's just a crash, Son, you'll be alright.

And how many more will there be? A lifetime of crashes. Alcohol, drugs. Wait 'til any of them slip down his throat, enter a vein, Jim thinks.

Outside, the dad picks up the remote control unit and points it, first at the car then the child's head. It doesn't work, he throws it away in disgust and frustration. Uses his foot to propel the car forward, every five metres he gives it another bored kick, shunts his baby's life along.

What Jim doesn't know and why would he? Was that this young man, this father, kicking his son down the street was ruined himself by the age of eight. Not only by his parents, even though they hadn't helped, but by a teacher, starting on his very first day at school. He'd picked up a pencil and for the first time in his very young life had started to make his mark. He'd held it out to a passing teacher, she'd looked at it, then at him, and without a word screwed it up and walked on, taking the pencil from his hand. The teacher had taught him for two years, worse than that, she had made sure of it. She was there at the start of the September term to greet and meet and ruin him for another year.

Shirley had wanted to move away from the area, precisely because of incidents like the one Jim has just witnessed or when their neighbour hung out an American flag. It just appeared and stayed up there, fluttering, until the red, white and blue had turned grey by storm and bird and it flapped itself slowly to death. He wasn't American and the chances he'd ever go there were remote, very remote, not unless America was looking for a topless man with hoops in his nipples and a can in his hand. He popped like a daffodil, was bare-chested from spring to the end of summer. She didn't like the area because of people like that and the buildings that were left to rot. The old church down the end of the street had been given over to pigeons and drunks, pigeons on roofs hooting, drunks huddled around doors hollering. All trying to make sense of each other's sermons. Seagulls giving it out on roofs, hackers leaning against walls, coughing, spitting it out on pavements. Shirley would have liked to have left the area years ago.

Jim was of a different opinion. It had been called and Jim had read this, Portobello on Sea. Unbeknown to Jim he'd been cutting hair for all this time on a potential gold mine. The antique shops arrived first and Jim had to admit that some of the stuff they found and sold was amazing. Then an estate agent came and shops selling bespoke, fancy homespun stuff. Norman Road was changing. Jim only had to look out of his window to see that. And looking out of the window is exactly what he was doing. He'd been trained in stillness, in the waiting game, the waiting of a head to be cut.

Well there it goes, Jim thinks, my New Year's resolution, to make an effort with my wife. It had sounded simple enough at the time. He'd made it after they'd kissed, a little good luck kiss, for another year at the ringing of the midnight bells. They'd gone to bed ten minutes later, taken to their sides, hadn't touched. They'd had nothing to say over Christmas or on New Year's night.

Obviously Shirley had different ideas, Jim thinks, standing with the card in his pocket, with the donkey staring up and out. The year ahead was looking longer and darker than in years. For the first time in his life, he wished he was blind, blind to the card, blind to what was to come. Instead of doing anything he stays where he is and gently taps on the window. If anyone could see him they'd think he was trying to get their attention. Maybe, as a welcome, maybe as a warning about the snow. Some might see him for what he was, a middle-aged man who'd just been left by his wife, tapping on a window for help. He didn't feel up to cutting hair, who'd come in anyway on a day like this? He didn't want to pull the blind, turn the sign from closed to open, plug in the trimmers or puff the air with a little white powder. He felt sick, sick in the pit of his stomach.

He was grateful for one thing, that his wife had been wise enough to strike while their son was away so he could at least get himself slightly sorted.

Where did it all go wrong?

Jim asks the window but it won't answer. When's a window ever given an answer to anything? And then he realises, probably plenty of times. One thing he really didn't like was the way Shirley treated him like a child, called him things like her good little helper. Treated him like someone who couldn't put his own boots on. He'd found it sweet in the early days, as an act of affection, then as the years went on, it had become condescending and annoying.

Chapter 3

As for their son, Luke, he flew home, the plane was so small and the toilet so close to the captain's back that Luke pushed harder than he'd ever pushed before. He didn't break through and hit the captain but he'd wanted to, he'd wanted to soak and ruin the pilot's blue jacket with his piss. He'd travelled home in a dug out seat that could be hosed down at the end of a working shift. The plane was like a flying tampon, a Ford Transit of the sky.

He hadn't realised his parents were having troubles. Why would he? He'd never really given them any thought at all. What did he care if his mum and dad were getting divorced? What was it to him? He'd heard arguments, some nights they'd forget to come in and say goodnight. Why'd they have to do that anyway? Who said goodnight and hello anymore? Most people he knew didn't even have both parents. The positive thing about it was that at least now he wasn't a freak. Freaks had two parents; it was bad enough that his mum was a teacher.

Luke had his own battles, it was a continuing war. Spots

appearing like molehills at night. It didn't matter how many he popped, they'd be back. Sometimes he just stood, looking at himself in the mirror, waiting, ready with his fingers. He'd caught one that way. He was like a hunter waiting over the seal's breathing hole. The spots were relentless, his face a battlefield. He was being attacked on all fronts, from top to bottom. He'd even started taking the contraceptive pill. He'd heard some girl saying they were good at clearing spots, some nights he took two. He was going to nuke the fuckers.

Worse than his spots was his voice. It made him sound like an ee-awing donkey and he knew it. He'd lost complete control of it; it went up and down, the frequency had busted. So he tried to keep quiet, used grunts instead of words. There was no other way of avoiding it.

Luke hated his face, hated his hair, hated school, hated that he looked like his parents, both of them. He was nearly six foot, useless as a newborn chick and worse than that, was the fact that he knew it.

On his first night home, as a treat, seeing as though Luke had decided to stay, they'd had a game of football in the front room as a celebration, used the settee as a five-a-side goal and smashed the mirror with Luke's first wayward kick. He didn't have a good shot, he was more of a goalie.

That's seven years of bad luck.

Jim said, regretting it as soon as the words were out.

Luke was at the age when the only things he could concentrate on were balls, bombs or bullets. Crossing a road was hazardous enough. He'd nearly been knocked over twice in the previous month. A man had had to do an emergency stop by his size twelve feet. What Luke couldn't do was concentrate. His fringe didn't help, didn't help his view of the world or his skin for that matter.

Luke decided to stick with his room, his posters, his Xbox, his dad.

What did he want to go and live with her for? She was a psycho.

The worst thing for Luke would be if his mum and dad didn't nail the split. He wanted it locked down water tight, signed and stamped. Secretly, he was well scared of his mum.

So you're sure? You're sure you're not going to get back together?

Jim had thought his son wanted them to make another go of it, was sending up a distress flair. Jim felt guilty, went over and ruffled his son's hair and made his apologies. Luke hated it when he did that, what was he, a bloody collie?

Chapter 4

Jim January cut hair. He was a barber, that's what he did and he was good at it. Cutting and trimming, didn't mind which. He used to share the barbers with another man, a partner who'd left to make his fortune in Malibu or some god awful sunny place. Where HP is served under a sweltering Spanish sky alongside a full english - the lot, the bangers, the bacon, the beans. Jim got a slurred, burped, bronzed answerphone message telling him how good life was, how he'd found his sunny Blighty, a gin and tonic fuelled paradise with a slice of lemon on top. They used to share a drink on a Friday night and a little natter, down the local Doom and Gloom.

Jim had thought about hiring someone but he hadn't as yet, hence the second empty chair.

If you wanted Jim to talk, he'd talk and if you didn't he wouldn't, it was up to the customer. He could do whatever you wanted. He could do the deep, the quick, or nothing at all, it was the customer's choice. None of it mattered to Jim. He'd worn the floor away with his shuffling around the chair. A regular, not a walk-in or a blow-in but a regular has just sat down for a chat.

Same as usual please.

Jim nods, tips the man's head forward and applies the apron, it flutters down. Looks at the man in the mirror. Jim knows he's got something to say, he usually does and doesn't take long before he says it.

Have I ever told you how much I hate our dog? It's a bastard, it thinks I'm the Messiah, bloody follows me everywhere.

Jim hadn't been told. Well, he doesn't think he has. The man says bastard, as if he's talking about a mugger.

I've hated it for years. It's my daughter's, should never have got it, but it was the only dream of hers I could bring alive, I'm a useless fucker, really.

Jim's always wondered what it would be like to be a shrink. What must they have to listen to? They'd have to come up with answers, Jim doesn't have to give those. He gets details as he snips behind the ear, some he probably shouldn't hear and some he rather wouldn't. Nothing's sacred as the apron goes round the neck, it's like a hangman's noose, they've got words to say.

You're going to think I'm nuts after you've heard this, might not even want me coming back.

The man laughs.

I doubt that.

Jim says.

I've managed to get rid of it, the dog.

Well, good for you.

Jim doesn't get into arguments with regulars, they wouldn't be back.

Do you want to know how?

Jim doesn't, but says:

Sure.

I've been shitting in the corner of the living room, when everyone went out.

Sitting?

No, shitting, poohing!

Oh.

Jim says.

When the coast was clear, so to speak, one shit a day,

never any more than that.

That's good.

Jim looks at the client in the mirror, same simple haircut for so many years. He's smiling as if he's talking about the weather or where he's going on his next sun-drenched holiday. Jim wonders why the rest of the family didn't pick up human scent, but doesn't mention it.

It took about a month, but he's out, the bastard's gone.

He says, getting excited as if he's talking about the birth of a new child. Jim doesn't have to say a thing, not a word. He keeps quiet but wonders who the real bastard is here.

I got the wife on side when I started doing the business on the bed. She loves our bed, clean sheets every Sunday. You know the type of woman.

So let me see if I got this right, that I haven't missed anything out, you started shitting on your own bed?

Jim didn't want any confusion. The man starts to nod. They're staring at each other in the mirror. Jim can't afford to give anything away, he doesn't allow his eyes to show their surprise, knows it's not just his hair cutting abilities which are on show when he's behind a man's back, it's also his listening ear.

Sure did. The dog's a goner. Some dog home has it now, Brighton way, I think.

He says, beaming.

And your daughter, what does she think?

Hasn't looked at or stroked a dog since, thinks they're disgusting, dirty creatures.

The man gives a thumbs-up to the mirror then goes silent, happy to have got it off his chest. Jim guesses it's something he'd not tell many people about. He gives Jim the note and says:

Take a little extra and keep it a secret.

Ask Jim about anything and he's got a little snippet. Want a story on tea? Jim's got one. Want one on biscuits? He's probably got one of those too. He's sure as hell got one on dogs now. Jim's got something a lot of people don't have, he's got stories. He's a fixture in the town, people recognise him, say hello and trust him. Doesn't matter what they're talking about, in the end all conversations come back to their hair. Jim's never met a man who isn't secretly paranoid that he'll lose it, see a bald patch appear. He sensed a lot by the way a customer slouched or sat, wriggled or stayed still. Jim could see what type of man you were by the aura around your head. He'd not told anyone that, not even his now departed wife. Jim really did think he could see different colours leaving the temples. Anger came out in black, love in red and ill health, yellow. Ask Jim, he saw the colour and he hadn't even read a book about it.

Jim didn't do fancy, didn't do streaks or perms. No, if it couldn't be done with scissors, combs or clippers, take your business elsewhere. He wasn't a stylist, more to the point, not a fussing around man. It had never been about the money he could put in his pocket. No, Jim liked the pace of barbering and the stories that came his way. He sure wasn't going to change. No, he left that to others, to do the fancy, leave the punter with the illusion that they'd just had the best haircut of their life because it had taken an hour of hand waffle.

Jim had been so stunned in the early stages of Shirley's departure, that Luke had been able to do pretty much whatever he'd liked. He'd joined a kickboxing club to toughen himself up, get hard, so he hoped. He'd been used as punch bag for four sessions, the only thing the other kids couldn't get was his head, which was so far up. It was only when he turned up with a note from Jim, pleading that they not hit his son so much, not because he couldn't take it (he couldn't) but because as a child he'd had meningitis and the battering had to stop. He'd been nicknamed M&M ever since. Luke thought he'd been named after the white rapper, a cool name. He hadn't, M&M stood for Meningitis Minger.

Jim went to work and Luke went to school, January soon became April and M&M gave up kickboxing because he wasn't up to it, he didn't have that knock out heart. Getting out of bed, pumping the blood up to his head was hard enough, shit, it gave him a headache.

Chapter 5

There'd been changes as the months passed.

Jim had taken on an apprentice, a boy, Danny. Back from the army, a tour in Iraq already under his belt, under his bonnet.

He was going to show him how to cut and two afternoons a week at college were going to do the rest.

It didn't really work out like that. Jim had more than tuition to give him. It didn't just involve cutting, the holding of the comb or scissors. He'd learnt that fast enough, he'd practiced and practiced and become efficient. He could twist and turn the comb and snip at the same time and make that clean cut rhythmical sound. His coordination was good, no problems there.

No, what Jim needed to teach him, what he needed to get across to Danny, was how not to invade people's personal space. He does it without knowing, stands a little too close, when he cuts or speaks. What Jim needed to teach him was respect for that invisible line. Jim senses how close his own cock gets to a customer's body, is careful not to let it brush or at least not linger too long.

How, he was ever going to teach him that, Jim didn't know. He'd never really thought about those subtleties, not until he'd met Danny who didn't have a clue. He came in over the comfort barrier, came that little bit too close, like a cat with its tail up. Jim was always stepping back when he spoke to Danny, customers did the same. Jim saw it in their eyes, they hit their personal space invaded button.

It was as if Danny's Wi-Fi was on the blink, his receptors not working right. Worse than that, was Danny's inability to relax. He'd stand erect, at attention by the empty chair, waiting for a command, like a guard guarding a gate at night. If he'd been a dog, his ears would have been pricked.

If Jim didn't say anything, didn't jog him, he'd stay like that, in his standing stupor, until the bell of the door rang. When Jim asked him about it, Danny had replied that in the army, you get told to stand still, remain silent and not to think.

I mastered all three to quite a high degree.

Danny joked, Jim didn't laugh but believed he had.

He'd only taken Danny on as a favour to Charlie Sloane.

They drank together on a Friday night at the Early Bird club, men drinking a pint to salute the end of the working week. They drank between five and seven o'clock then returned home with conversation, drinking and darts inside, a dying breed now. It wouldn't be long before his own son might need a helping hand. It felt right to put a bit of goodwill out there, so Jim had.

The thing Danny really lacked was confidence. It was missing. Jim had noticed it pretty early on.

Only yesterday, Jim had read in the local paper about a woman who gave weekend charisma classes. One thousand pounds is what it would cost for the un-charismatic to fix their charisma magnet. Well, if you could teach charisma, Jim had thought, then personal space awareness shouldn't be such a problem.

Jim had cut Danny's hair as a youngster, he'd sit quietly in his chair as Jim and Charlie talked. A well-mannered kid, if a little shy. As he got older he'd started coming in on his own, his favourite football team's scarf around his neck.

Jim cut his hair before he went away to war. After it was done, Jim had said and he'd never forget it, never get over his embarrassment (it was another reason he'd taken him on, to amend for what he'd said).

No charge, have it on me, now go and bag yourself one.

Is what he'd said. What he had meant to say was:

No charge, have it on me, is your bag packed?

Jim still doesn't know why he'd said it. But while he was cutting, as it was getting shorter, he'd wanted something profound, something wise to say. Truth be told Jim felt guilty. He was of that lucky generation who'd not had to fight in any war and who were now too old and useless to ever be asked.

He shouldn't have worried, Danny hadn't heard a word. He'd been far too pent up and sick, thinking about his tomorrows.

Jim never mentioned it again. He thought it was something they shared, an embarrassment that neither of them would ever mention.

In truth, Jim liked the kid, old before his time was the saying that might best sum him up.

Danny told occasional war stories slowly, his flashbacks, over sandwiches out the back, by the kettle. Where customers weren't allowed to go, near the computer Danny had asked to bring in so he could have Skype conversations with his friend in New Zealand. They talked about lost body parts over chocolate digestives.

In some ways he was older, more experienced in life than Jim himself, he may have had stories, an understanding of a head and the set of shoulders it belonged on, but Danny had already put his young life on the line and seen bullets hit shoulders and heads.

Imagine the worst shit you can be in and then double it. That's where I took myself, did it of my own accord.

He'd come out with things like that. Jim didn't have to ask. They'd just slip out. Another time he talked about this hole he'd dug and how he ended up living in it for a week, taking direct fire. How he'd shivered and cried and for the first time since he could remember hadn't written in his diary, because he couldn't keep control over his hand.

Night after night the sky roared.

You're sounding more and more like John Wayne.

Jim replied.

Again he didn't know what to say, knew he wanted to keep things light. Danny looked at him and blankly said.

Who's that?

God, Jim thought, realising how young Danny was.

How quickly things are forgotten. Everything, from old film stars to wars, everything forgotten, the agenda relentlessly moving on. The Duke dead and now forgotten as is Nam, Korea, as would be Iraq and Afghanistan. Wouldn't be long before an SS outfit at a fancy dress party was as common as a nurse's, no-one remembering what they stood for, just that they looked good on a pair of young shoulders.

Jim secretly thanked Danny for being a welcome distraction.

It saved him thinking about his own predicament, his burnt out marriage and the failure of that. It kept him off his own back. It was either learn the piano or go see a shrink. Jim had thought about doing both, but as yet hadn't taken a step forward in either direction.

He'd pretty much taken on Danny after the split. It made him feel that he was doing something worthwhile with his life. He was glad that his chosen profession hadn't been an utter waste. That he did indeed have something useful to teach and pass on.

More importantly was the realisation that the shit in his own life hadn't blown in, hadn't started to bubble and burst until he was middle aged and maybe more able to take it. That he wasn't carrying Danny's load at such an age. Because that's what Danny carried, a load of hurt, it was in his eyes, on his shoulders, the way he came in a little too close.

Danny asks Jim on arriving at the barbers with his fishing rods still dripping sea spray:

What's the point of all this Jim?
And he makes a sweeping gesture with his hand. Jim hopes he isn't just talking about the barbers.

None, but maybe it's later than you think?

He'd always liked the song, liked the words and was glad to have found it deep in his recesses. He's at an age when he forgets things, goes back to his larder of a memory and there's nothing but empty space where preserve jars of past events were once stored. Jim hates that, the dark emptiness of his larder.

Yeah, I guess you're right.

Danny replied.

But he didn't seem convinced. What Jim knew for sure, was that he was dealing with a wounded soul, something ticking, deep inside. It was only a hunch. He never discussed it with Charlie Sloane when they were sharing a Friday drink.

He wasn't going to tell him:

Yeah, your son's an accident waiting to happen, a bomb already primed.

He'd asked how his son was doing, how he was coping, getting on with it all. Jim lied, what else could he do? He was good at holding back truths.

He's fine. Have his own boutique before long, you wait and see, be taking business from me.

Charlie had always worried about his youngest, he hadn't done as well at school as he might. In Charlie's eyes his son just wasn't pushy enough, wasn't as a child, doesn't seem to be as a young man, had always been in the background, letting his older brother take centre stage.

The biggest surprise of all had been him signing up, he hadn't seen that coming and neither had his wife. Danny hadn't asked his parents for approval, there'd been no discussion, no advice. Secretly, Charlie had thought it would be the making of him. Not that he'd come back with some sort of disorder and Charlie didn't mean the clap. The Sloanes weren't embarrassed, they were more than happy just to have him intact, they'd seen enough disturbing images on the news and pictures in papers to know how lucky they were.

Danny's mate, Carl, Skyped him weekly. To Jim's annoyance it always seemed to be in the middle of a cut. He didn't like thinking that way and corrected himself when he did. He didn't want to be tight, his own father had been that. One miser in any family was more than enough. He'd always tried to fight against it, but it didn't stop him from flicking switches off at home.

The Skyping always affected Danny, did something to his mood. He'd be laughing, more alive than at any other time during the day, pulling silly faces, showing his scissors, performing for the Skype world. But afterwards, once his friend had been clicked away, he'd become quieter, more introspective, sadness seeped out. Sadness was what Danny had by the bucket, like a virus, an infection, something deep in the vein. The sad thing for Jim was that he thought he saw it in his own son.

Carl had flown away minus a leg, a going away present from Iraq and the tour. He'd gone to live in New Zealand, to be as far from the war as he could, to find open space, space to think. Space his friend back in the UK should also find and grab.

Jim had overheard it mentioned in conversation.

Shit Jim, I could go out there pretty soon and learn how to shear. Never know I might be good at it.

Danny said.

Jim wasn't sure if he was joking:

You reckon you're good enough for sheep already?

I reckon I've done a fair few already.

Jim had to agree with Danny, that perhaps he had. That perhaps he'd already sheared a field full. Jim knew for sure he'd sheared a whole valley, maybe more than that.

The more Danny heard from his one legged friend the more he wanted to go, to go and get some of that space. And the thing about it was that it grew stirrings in Jim as well.

You be careful out there.

Danny said, ending a Skype call. Carl had just told him about a farmer who'd driven his car out into the middle of the field in the mountains amongst his sheep and the sky, covered his car in a beautiful, expensive, rose print blanket and blown his long-haired head off. The suicide note had been tucked away in a plastic wallet. Said he hoped there wouldn't be too much mess to clean. He'd marked his favourite sheep, to give as a personal present to his godson (reckoned it would be a good breeder). He'd lost his wife to lung cancer the week before, she was dead within a month of diagnosis. He couldn't see the point of going forward and sure wasn't going to go to her funeral or give up smoking himself.

Jim got a little anxious when Danny sat down to Skype now, didn't want anymore surprises coming his apprentice's way.

Jim has a motorbike, he's had if for years, he'd always wanted to see some of that space Carl talked about. Preferably he'd like to ride himself all the way there. He'd never done a trip, not as yet. He'd bought the bike brand new years ago, he'd hardly used it. He remembers the day he bought it, 1st of August over twenty years ago now, proud as punch. It has sat there in the garage ever since. He still looks at it, it still makes him turn his head.

Cluttering up the place.

Was how Shirley first referred to it for a year or two, then as the albatross around his neck. Finally, she called it that thing, Jim knew what she thought of it by the way she said it. Shirley knew exactly the type of child who went on to ride mopeds, kill themselves squeezing that last bit of testosterone out of the throttle. She didn't want any part of it. Jim could have his silly, open-ended dreams, all she asked was that he wouldn't share them with her, especially, not after they had their son.

Jim had bought the bike before Luke was born, before he'd even been a twinkle, with the aim of riding it around the world or at least somewhere in the world. His parents, brother and friends had all laughed. He didn't have a licence, never had a scooter, had never straddled an engine with two wheels before. They said he'd never do it, kept other nastier thoughts quiet, like he didn't have it in him, didn't have the bottle. That he was a home bird and always would be. That he wouldn't do anything without his wife and that they all knew who wore the trousers in his house.

Things were said. What they didn't know was that Jim had a plan, had for years. It was another good reason why Jim cut hair, so he'd have a trade wherever he went and one for when he got back. He'd wanted his wife to travel with him, well, he had before. She'd been substituted for his son now. In fact he didn't want his wife anywhere near the bike in case she jinxed him and it.

Anyway, as the years rolled by, people forgot about Jim's dreams, his nonsense trip, his around the world plan. Of course they had, they had their own lives, dreams, obsessions to be getting on with or avoiding, whatever it was most people did with their lives. Jim never really knew. He knew he'd done a lot of avoiding in his. Some don't explore or search for truths, they stay still or stop with the little knowledge they've acquired and are comforted by that.

Well, that wasn't enough for Jim, even if others thought it was. That's what had attracted him to his teacher, the knowledge inside her head: he'd wanted to tap that. Well, he had at first. Now his bike was his reminder. Every time he went into the garage and flicked the light, it sat there as a silent red metal reminder of who or what he might become, if he could muster up the time, the courage.

Every year he'd drop the oil, check the fluids and make sure it was ready to ride. Every two years he'd put a new battery in. It had to be ready, ready for Jim and his dream. It was his private fire engine, waiting in the dead of the night to take him and his son away. Shirley stopped mentioning the albatross around his neck, that thing, just taking up space.

Subtle changes, Jim heard them and Shirley liked making them.

Chapter 6

Shirley had got herself into Latin dance and found a wandering finger trying to hitch her skirt.

She'd thought that was where it was snaking. Shocked, she'd removed it and put it back where it belonged, on her hip to guide her along in the dance. She couldn't be sure if he'd done it on purpose or if it was a slip, a lack of concentration. Her dance partner was seventy years of age and she'd let him off, just this once, thought that he'd grabbed her for balance or misplaced a foot. But when he had another go the following week, she'd moved her foot onto his and pushed hard. She wouldn't be dancing with him again and he'd left the dance floor with an imprint in his shoe and a suffering toe.

She was trying to get out more, be more sociable, pretend that she was a woman on the mend. She sometimes went for a drink after the dancing and found herself talking about his behaviour.

Oh him, he's known as the Wanderer.

Why doesn't anyone say anything?

To tell you the truth he can't hear. I think he's nearly deaf and we need men to make up the numbers.

It's not his hearing I'm worried about, it's his hands.

Shirley had to admit he was one of the better gentleman dancers, if she could call him that.

The following week she waited for the old man to leave the lesson, got him while he was alone. She wouldn't have wanted to embarrass him, not in front of others. She'd learnt that at school, to do the telling off in private, behind a door, it was better that way. She wasn't going to break a habit of a lifetime. She walked up to him and mouthed hello. He nodded his head in acknowledgement and before he could move she took his wayward hand and scolded him like a kid, wagging her finger an inch from his face. Others might let him get away with it, but she certainly wouldn't. God knows where it could lead. She'd always thought bad behaviour needed to be stamped out, squashed in fact. He'd thought her a feisty woman, with a tasty rump. He might be an old-timer but he wasn't done and dusted yet.

She'd been surprised by Luke's decision to stay with his dad but accepted it, what else could she do? She'd been the one that had flown the nest. She wouldn't push him, sure wouldn't punish him, no, she'd wait, she was always there if he needed her helping hand. She'd never been an overbearing mum, but she did look forward to her Wednesdays and Thursdays with Luke. She liked to know how he and his education were getting on, if he was making the most of it. He wasn't.

Her flat was taking shape, she'd spent time choosing it and was happy with its isolated location and lack of neighbours. Miss Petticoat was doing well, the tears, the worries had stopped months ago. It was obvious now that the decision had been correct. Her relationship with Jim was already cordial, if a little curt. Not one argument, not a bad word, sure they had choppy waters to cross, but they'd cross them, like the adults they were.

Chapter 7

Luke liked saying hello to a dog as he walked to school.

Dogs were loyal, they didn't fuck you around. Something as simple as that had become the best thing of his day. He'd even bend, when he had the energy, and stroke it. The same couldn't be said about his laces as they bounced off the pavement. Some mornings it felt to Luke as if sleep had sapped his energy rather than topped it up, he didn't know what he did when he was asleep but it sure tired him out. He'd dreamed last night that he was on an iceberg and it was drifting in the Atlantic, somewhere cold. Luke was alone and he'd gone hoarse shouting for help as a large penguin tried to mount him. He had this beady, sneaky yellow eye and his breath smelt of mackerel. Luke woke in a sweat as the penguin started to snog him.

Every morning Luke hates himself a little more. He knew what he had to do, he had to bloody well cheer up. More importantly he needed to make some frigging friends. He hated walking around as a Johnny. Everyone else seemed so figured, so sussed, so fucking cool.

They were all in tight groups, huddled and bundled, laughing. He was jealous. He felt excluded, not by them, but by how he felt about himself. Luke giggles when he's nervous, he hates it. It bugs him, so he mopes around on the outskirts, never really knowing how to get in.

Ollie's talking to his crew, he's popular, he's always been popular, he's talking about the joys of becoming a father, he's just found out. Luke had been a friend of Ollie's once, in the inner group, not now. An ocean of coolness is between them now, not even a nod. So he's on the outside staring over heads, listening to Ollie bragging.

I can't fucking well believe it! I don't know if I'm ready for this type of shit or not. Me? A fucking dad!

His posse looked on and Luke knew the answer to that question. He knew the bloody answer, alright. No fucking way. Luke couldn't understand how he'd become a father, with his acne. One positive thing about it, Luke thought, it gave him a hell of a chance.

On hearing the news, Luke had made a pact with himself to knock on the door of a girl who he sometimes walked to school with, Molly. Most of the kids lived the other side of town, not Molly. Somehow Luke's mum had managed to get him into a school that perhaps he wasn't quite entitled to, he wished she hadn't, it would have saved him the bloody walk.

He'd occasionally Facebook the girl and had been round to hers before, he hoped she'd let him in. She did, but not before crushing him with:

What are you doing here?

Said with such indifference, that she couldn't have been less welcoming.

Ollie's going to be a dad.

Luke giggled.

Durr, everyone knows that.

Molly knew the mother. She'd raise her top and let anyone in the school touch her imagined bump. There wasn't one yet, but that didn't stop a girl thinking she'd felt the sperm squirming. The mother had become Queen Bee for the day. She wasn't normally so popular but opening her legs had changed that for twenty-four hours.

She'd always been surprised by how quickly it ended. She'd only just close her eyes or remove her brace before it was over. She didn't know what all the fuss was about really. Easy peasy, lemon squeezy was how she'd described sex to a particularly close friend.

Luke was allowed through Molly's door but it didn't mean they had much else to say. It would have helped matters if they had. Nothing, not a dickey, he racked his brain, but he couldn't think of one other thing to say. Luke followed Molly upstairs. He hopes his pants are clean. She opens the door and they enter her room and then the awkwardness really starts. She sits down on her bed and carries on with her computer, tapping away, talking to her mates in Facebook world. Plugging in her earphones, cutting him out and off. He'd given up on Facebook, it was depressing and watching her do it was worse. It was no spectator sport. Molly doesn't look at Luke, just keeps looking deep into the flickering world.

Luke manages ten minutes of the tedium and then stands up, yawns, stretches his gangling limbs and knocks the overhead light. He's going to say something and then thinks, what's the bloody point? Home's better than this.

See ya, then.

He says.

Oh, bye.

Without looking up or taking her eyes off the screen. Luke then remembers why he came.

Do you want to go steady?

Molly looks up, sighs.

Yeah, alright.

She then goes back to her computer, to announce to her 532 friends that she and Luke January were going steady. She doesn't get a totally favourable response from her postings, but it gives Molly four hours of bombardments to answer.

Luke was happy he'd got hitched. He couldn't wait to finger her and perhaps sit on her face and do some right disgusting things to her. He didn't care what. Everyone at school was talking about it and doing it, he wanted to do it so much he'd started dreaming of sex with penguins. He was going to give her a right Red Bull seeing to. That was Luke's drink of choice at the moment, Red Bull, no wonder he couldn't sleep and his teeth were rotting. Under his bed was a blue, white and red can graveyard. His room had taken on a very, sickly sweet scent.

Jim January wasn't a good cook by any stretch. He didn't really enjoy it, found it hard to keep up with all the boiling, frying and burning, harder if he was trying to read a recipe at the same time. That didn't mean they hadn't been eating, they had, mostly takeaways. He'd put weight on since Shirley had left, so he'd gone on the Atkins diet. Everyone seemed to be on it or talking about it. It seemed contagious. Jim had a regular who came in sucking a sausage as a man would a cigar. Jim had thought he was trying to quit smoking, he wasn't.

Why the sausage?

Jim asked, it would have been rude not to and the smell

of it was making him feel hungry.

To keep the chill away from my hunger.

The regular said he was going through twenty-four packs of sausages a week and this was the point, there was this miracle happening, he was still shedding the weight. The man couldn't believe it and nor could Jim. So Jim was now eating a cow and a pig a day and he'd started shedding. He'd thought that if he kept eating meat at this rate, he'd have to start driving out to the country, start to do some serious rustling, come back with a van full of beasts. He'd been told about the carbohydrate thing, but he still didn't get it, not really. It didn't seem to make any sense to Jim. He was eating a beast a day and the weight was dropping. It was only when he went from fourteen stone to ten in one day that he realised his scales were seriously dodgy. That in fact he'd only lost two pounds. Truly he'd been relieved, he'd eaten more parts of an animal in ten days than he thought was humanly possible, he was sure the hairs on his arms were getting coarser, more pig-like in fact, any more meat and he'd be growing hooves and walking on all fours.

So to celebrate the fact he wasn't a hyena he invited his young apprentice over for pizza. Fuck it, he'd throw caution to the wind and have some bloody carbs, give up on that meat thing. He'd order garlic bread as well.

Danny didn't do much at nights, he spent most of his time at home, writing. Jim wondered what he wrote about but never asked, didn't want to pry, didn't want to be nosy. Secretly though, he thought it must be some sort of Andy McNab, *Bravo Two Zero* soldier adventure. When Danny did go out, it had led to incidents. He was a returned warrior, a big fish in a very small pond. There were young men who thought he was fair game to have a pop at. He wasn't, he wasn't that type of young man at all.

Jim decided he was going to do his old party trick with the tablecloth to cheer Luke and Danny up. His intention was to pull it off, leaving the plates and glasses unmoved. He'd never managed it, that wasn't the point. He liked doing it. The not succeeding made it funny, the mayhem, the mess. Luke needed some cheering, he'd dipped again. (On returning from Molly's he'd taken up Facebook again and checked his status to find out he'd been dumped. He'd not even got a kiss in, never mind a finger.)

If Luke had looked at the table he might have noticed that he'd never seen the plates or glasses before but he wasn't that sort of attentive boy. It was all charity stuff, bought for the trick. Everything would be smashed, shattered on the floor, the trick would cost Jim two pounds at most. If it made Luke laugh it was money well spent, hoped that Danny would do the same.

He shouted to them:

Here boys, I've got a trick. I'm going to remove this

tablecloth from the table leaving everything else in place. Now watch carefully, you two, this is bloody brilliant.

The boys stared as Jim ripped the cloth away in one quick jerky movement. Everything went up, then came down hitting the table, smashing to the floor.

After a moment of embarrassment for his boss, Danny followed Luke in his laughter. He really did think that Jim had cocked up or gone mad. He couldn't imagine his own dad doing something so stupid.

The worst thing about the trick for Jim was cleaning up all the bloody glass. It went everywhere but he'd always thought it worth it, even if it took him half an hour of painstaking cleaning.

He'd first done it one Christmas, just for Shirley, to impress her, to have a bit of a laugh. She'd looked at him as if he was a stranger then looked on through him as if he wasn't there. Explaining the trick hadn't helped, she hadn't wanted to know. She'd moaned for the rest of the day because she'd got a piece of glass stuck in her foot, which she was sure needed hospital treatment. It hadn't, but it didn't stop her from moaning.

Amazing how many years I spent with a woman I probably shouldn't have.

Wasted time, Jim thinks.

It was the same when he'd started bringing bags of hair clippings home to compost in the garden, to mulch around the plants. He'd heard it was good for them, a punter had said it added nutrients to the soil. She'd looked at him in utter disbelief, then later as he was emptying it out, digging it in, blonde, black, brown and silver, as if he was a stranger, as if she didn't know him at all.

I don't want other people's hair floating around my garden, it's disgusting.

He hadn't listened, he kept bringing it home, digging it in, by God he had some hair buried under the plants in his garden.

Jim had worried his son would be awkward, shy around Danny. They'd only met once before at the barbers, months back and that was a slow nod. He needn't have worried. Jim doesn't know this, it's not important enough for Luke to have told him but he goes fishing some mornings with Danny, quite a lot of mornings. He'd been doing so for months. Luke saw Danny as a living REAL LIFE hero, believed he was sitting a metre away from a killer. He couldn't conceal his curiosity any longer, he'd wanted to ask it for a while when they were fishing but really he needed the safety of being near his dad to ask it.

Have you, you know, have you ever killed anyone, Danny?

Says it like the teenager he is, with his pizza (no olives) sticking out of his mouth, he hates olives, they make him feel sick. It's about the longest sentence Jim has heard his son utter in months.

A whole sentence, Jim thinks.

Danny looks at Jim, wants to check if it's alright to answer. Jim shrugs his shoulders, raises his eyes, as if to say why not?

Well, I once cut a man's ear off.

Wow. You fucked him right up, what did he do?

He sort of screamed and sobbed. No, of course I didn't really Luke, I was always a crap shot, I never hit anything and definitely didn't cut any ears off.

Jim's glad he said that. He wouldn't want his son getting any wrong ideas. Wouldn't want him signing up, or going around cutting people's ears off. Jim's noticed how politicians weren't sending their sons and daughters off to fight; he'd already done a Google check. How they talked about honour and nation, yet when it came to it, they weren't ready to send their loved ones off to die and it sickened Jim. Danny's own battle scars were manifestation enough of going to war.

Jim cleaned up and watched the boys playing Xbox. He can't see Danny any other way, than as a boy.

I know he's twenty-one but by God, Jim thinks, he's really just a boy.

The Xbox had come out of Luke's bedroom when Shirley left. It was a way in which Jim could spoil his son and keep an eye on him at the same time, clever parenting, he'd thought. Jim had tried playing but he kept on getting killed, much to Luke's annoyance, so Luke banned him from playing. Shirley would never have allowed it. She hated the noise and what she thought it did to the young, all that violence entering their putty-like minds.

He'd been watching them play for half an hour. He couldn't believe that there were only seven years between them.

You're well minging.

Luke says, winning another game. Danny pushes him, then rolls on top and pins him down, starts battering him with a cushion. Jim looks at them.

Hey Danny, I've got an idea you might be interested in.

Jim offers.

Oh yeah, what's that?

Danny says, whacking Luke again.

Why don't you borrow my bike? Ride it all the way

to New Zealand, it'd be one hell of an adventure and you've got somewhere to go when you arrive.
I'd put money on it making it.

The boys stop wrestling.

Luke's puffing, he hasn't moved so much in months, Jim's sure he puffs turning in his sleep.

Jim hadn't planned the offer, it just came out. Maybe it was the time to pass on his travelling dream. He's not sure, but he's offered it now, it's out in the open.

Here, I'll show you it.

Jim's excited. They walk out to the garage and the three of them stand in a line, looking at it, under the flickering fluorescent light. To Jim it looks beautiful. He's never fallen out of love with it, likes its lines, its style. To the boys it looks old and vintage.

So, what do you think? It's been waiting around long enough to see a bit of this world.

Jim hadn't even known he was going to offer it, not until he'd opened his mouth and now here he was getting all poetic. He surprised himself. He's enjoying himself, enjoying the night with the boys.

I'm sorry, Jim, I don't even have a licence.

Danny says.

He looks young again, made nervous by the offer.

You'd easily get one, look at the idiots already on the road. I didn't have one when I bought the Rocket.

Rocket?

That's what I call her.

Jim suddenly feels guilty that he'd never told Luke its name nor spoken to him about his dream. They'd stayed locked in the garage and in his head, his heart, for years. Maybe there wasn't a right time to tell a son of your stalled dreams? Maybe that's what good fathers don't do. Don't go on about what they could have done, should have done.

It's something I've always wanted to do, get on that bike and ride it. You can do it, you don't have any responsibilities.

Danny knows that but it doesn't make what's going on in his mind any easier.

Jim has a map of the world, a big laminated one. Most nights when he's brushing his teeth, he looks at it, dreams a little. Runs his finger across it and makes a very low broom, broom, noise. He never liked Shirley hearing this childlike sound, yet when he looked at a place he wanted to go to he couldn't help himself. She'd caught him more than once. There was a time, years ago now, when he could name all the countries in Africa, starting from the bottom going up, left to right, ocean to ocean. He hoped that the map would inspire his son with a bit of wonder. Give him names of places where he might want to go. He'd shown him the Alps before he went off skiing and now after going upstairs he's showing the two of them where New Zealand and Carl are.

It's about twelve thousand miles, when you get there you've gone as far as you can before you're heading back.

Danny might have been to war, left men in a burial hole, but he hadn't known where New Zealand really was.

Jim didn't know if it was Danny walking into his life or Shirley walking out but something odd was happening. What's a life if you do no good? What's the point? He'd thought about becoming a Samaritan, doing something, driving the blind around one morning a week or doing a bit of respite care. Doing something. He'd made telephone calls, made mistakes when giving out his post code. That's T for Tits, N for Nutter, 0 for zero U for Uganda, reckoned he'd covered all the bases for being rude and abusive. Jim knew he'd have to sort out how to say his postcode before he'd be welcome in the volunteer community.

Anyway it's up to you Danny, no pressure, if you want it,

it's yours. I'll help you plan the route, get the visas and the insurance sorted out.

Jim says, leaving the bathroom, turning from the map, pulling the light.

The boys went back to killing and Jim watched, with a cup of tea, from his chair. After Danny had gone, Luke said:

You're alright really, Dad. Can we look at the map again?

Sure.

Jim's surprised, pleased about his son's curiosity and they go back upstairs and look over the map. (Luke had heard earlier that Molly had decided not to dump him after all.)

Jim thinks it's the most responsive he's been in months. What was he usually? A grunting, head shaking, monosyllabic, eyes too tired to lift, disinterested, self-obsessed kid. Couldn't say he didn't love him though.

Thanks, Son, it's good to have you back.

Jim replied and ran his hands through his son's hair, irritating Luke.

What do you mean, back?

Well, you hardly say a thing anymore.

Jim didn't want to change the ambience in the room, but thinks he already has.

Why'd you call it the Rocket?

I guess I hoped it would take me somewhere, like a rocket, off to another planet and in its day it was pretty fast.

Shirley had hated the ugly laminated map hanging in the bathroom and had asked Jim on numerous occasions to remove the bloody thing. She could swear occasionally.

How many times have I asked you?

She'd say, looking at him and it in the mirror, as they brushed away at teeth. Shirley was good at brushing, she'd already rubbed away her enamel, the dentist had told her to stop brushing so hard. They'd been through two maps in their marriage. He sure wasn't going to hang it down in the garage.

You're a teacher aren't you? Well, what's a map on a wall if not an educational tool?

He liked using that one, it did the trick every time. It kept his wife away from his map.

Chapter 8

Danny left Jim's house thinking about New Zealand, thinking about his friend. Full of hope for the future, it didn't last, good feelings rarely did for Danny anymore.

He wasn't going anywhere, not on Jim's motorbike or on foot and he knew it. It was two hundred metres down the road before the black clouds swooped in and took any good feelings away. His stride started to slow to a stop. He hadn't taken his night medication, his pills, hadn't taken them for two days. Not since he went out with his brother, Joseph, for a drink, not something he'd have normally done or want to do. He thought he'd meet him on level terms, eye to eye, as a returning solider, as a brother looking for answers. He hadn't met him on those terms, not at all. His confidence crumbled as their eyes met and he offered his hand. Joseph shook it and then took full control, as he always did, guiding the conversation.

You and I should spend more time together.

It wasn't said with brotherly love, Danny knew what

he meant. Joseph talked, laughed and kept grinning and poking, Danny wasn't there to listen to Joseph, he was there for answers. He was the one who should be talking. He'd been thinking about this for years, turning the question upside down, inside out, this way and that. He sat stewing as his brother got the next round in and then the one after that. Danny had thought he'd be able to confront his brother now but he hadn't, it all stayed locked inside. Three years of thinking and turning it over and he still couldn't let the words come.

His brother dictated, directed, dominated all of the silences with his patter.

Danny left the pub far worse than he'd arrived, nothing had changed. Everything remained the same. He was left with dark thoughts, fear and the realisation that he would never be able to confront his brother. That he had again lost.

The last beating he'd taken haunts him, it was worse than the ones before, more frenzied, savage. Three years. He wakes with it and sleeps on it.

Fancy coming home and beating the shit out of my brother?

How had he known he'd receive a favourable answer from a stranger, how did one psycho recognise another?

Did he ask it at the start of the night, over the first pint?

How many people had he needed to ask? How many pints needed to be sunk? Was he turned down? Was he sweating or smiling when he asked? Was he anxious, legs shaking? Was he looking straight into the other man's eyes?

Or, did he wait, asking leading questions, taking his time until he was sure he'd found an accomplice, the right man, the right nutter? How long had it taken? A week, a month, a year? Was he a Facebook friend or someone found in the small-ads? Was he worried the man might turn, snitch, before or after the beating? Had it been planned or had it been spontaneous?

Had he paid the man? Paid him up front or waited to see if the man had the stomach? Was it the first time for the other man? Had he enjoyed it, gone home elated?

Danny had heard the shoes coming, the front door slamming, the running up the stairs, he hadn't had time to tremble, time to get out of the bath. Joseph had kicked in the door. Without a word one leather gloved punch after another. Held under, pulled up and pushed under, up and down he went, head bouncing off the bottom, the sides. Danny, fighting for his life, losing consciousness, coming to. Finally dragged from the bath, kicked a few more times, left naked and bleeding on the floor.

Had the stranger been talked into it by Joseph? Coerced? Had they laughed about it? Gone for another drink? Had they said goodbye at the door and shaken on it, hugged?

Had they tipped their heads in acknowledgement of their achievement? Did they do it to others? Does his brother still see the man? Did they brag about it or was it a secret? Does the other man still think about it? Did he ever think about it?

So many questions and he couldn't ask one.

It had taken two months for his body to heal and the swelling to subside. He told his parents he'd been attacked by a stranger (a bit of that was true) they'd been away at a wedding. The truth was told to his diary, locked away in a suitcase, he'd long ago stopped sharing that with his parents.

Always writing in that bloody thing.

His dad had moaned once.

One little throwaway sentence like that and Danny's diary disappeared from view.

Getting home from Jim's, Danny said hello and goodnight to his mum and dad without pausing for breath or stopping at their door. They hardly noticed, they were coming to the end of a film they were enjoying, they'd seen it before, that didn't matter, it made the ending clearer. He climbed the stairs and went into his room, closed his door. He walked over to his desk, switched on the anglepoise, unlocked his diary, put the key on top of a blank piece of paper and started to write, as he had done since he was young. His mum bought him a diary every year. She knew he used them, she hated waste, she was a thrifty, thirties child.

He took time from the lines to sharpen two pencils. He'd always written with one, did so in Iraq, did so here. He inserted one into each nostril, he'd do that when he was thinking, bored, liked them hanging there, liked twisting them gently round and around, in and out, feeling the inside of his nostril, it tickled. He'd always done it, started at school, teachers used to tell him to take them out, as had his parents. He's sitting there bouncing the lead, the pencils going up and down in his nostrils.

Danny rocks back on his chair, closes his eyes in thought. Then propels himself forward banging the pencils into the table, driving them in. They went up through his nose into his nasal passages, through the membrane, piercing his brain. His parents were at the end of their film when their son hit the floor.

What was that?

His mum asked, as the credits began to roll.

The End.

Charlie Sloane said, clapping his hands. He was more right than he'd ever been before, it was indeed The End for his son.

Chapter 9

Miss Petticoat, Shirley, didn't know how she got to have an audience, a one to one with the wandering hand, but she had. She couldn't blame it on anything, not the wine, not the tea she'd poured. Couldn't have been a date drug. Could it? What would a man of his age be doing going around with that in his pocket? No.

She's finding it hard to concentrate on the Sunday paper, hard to get the coffee down, finding it hard to do anything but think about last night. Last night couldn't even be classified as unfaithful, going behind her husband's back. No, she and Jim had split, it was final, had been months now. But with a man old enough to be her father, a man seventy years old?

Honest to God, she thinks. What's wrong with me? She's shocked herself.

Shirley's found that since the break up, her friends, more precisely her female friends (she hasn't many) haven't been as warm, not as giving as she thought she'd have been in the same situation. Some hadn't returned calls or invited her over or out. She'd started turning up uninvited and could see it in their eyes. The way they'd take a husband's hand when she entered the room, they wouldn't have before. Was it that she'd become a threat, someone to watch? A single woman out on the prowl? Or maybe a catalyst for marital dissatisfaction? She'd been surprised by the lack of sisterly love, perhaps it was her own paranoia. That had been levelled at her more than once before.

She didn't know if it was compassion, the wine or maybe a mixture of the two, when she'd taken the wanderer's dancing hand and led him to the sheets.

She'd found out that his deafness was a bit of idle gossip. He'd had one of his eardrums go on his sixtieth birthday, the other worked perfectly well.

I couldn't hear much with two good ears. You can imagine how deaf I am now.

She liked the way he talked without self-pity and the way he'd been gentle, stroking and slow, took his time. More importantly he'd made her laugh and she hadn't been doing much of that of late. She was a bit anxious about strokes and heart attacks.

How the hell would I explain this? She thought. How would I explain having a pensioner in my bed? He'd be too heavy to shift by myself, she couldn't have called

Jim or Luke to help.

He'd looked at her as if sensing her mood, her thoughts and said:

I've a piece of good news to tell you.

She'd waited, thinking it would be about his pacemaker. She was sure she could feel something, like a lump in the dark, where a heart would normally pump. She really had patted around for wires as if he was a ticking bomb.

I'm not seventy for a couple of months yet, I'm still relatively young, in my sixties.

Shirley had laughed, he had gripped her hands and added:

I just thought you should know that I'm probably good for another go.

And by God, he was. Shirley bets her pensioner would be good at direction, good with a map because he sure was good at positions she'd never been in or thought about before.

Who would have guessed? Shirley thought as they went back for seconds.

Chapter 10

Jim was cutting hair, listening to the exploits of one of his older clients when he got the news from Charlie Sloane, his voice so quiet on the end of the phone that he'd hardly been able to make out the word 'dead'. Charlie had said it so softy, so painfully. But that's what Jim had heard, Danny's dead.

He didn't need to be told that again. The boy who'd stood there yesterday on parade, in front of these very same mirrors, who stared out the window waiting for a head was now dead.

Jim carried on cutting, listening to the man's story in front of him, but he didn't have the ear for it now. He didn't do the follow round with the mirror. No, he wanted both the client, and the man waiting, to disappear. Most of all, he needed silence, time to think, time to consider, to sit down, to stand up, make his tea, or not.

I'm sorry, Tom, I've just had some terrible news. Would you mind coming back another day?

Jim didn't care if he did or didn't. He wasn't in the mood for cutting, wasn't going to be cutting his or anyone else's hair for the rest of the day or maybe longer than that. The man tried to say something, Jim turned his back and walked away, didn't care if he lost his custom or not.

After they'd left, he covered his and Danny's chair with a big blue bib as a mark of respect, nodded to the mirrors and dropped a tear. Then went out back, pushed the kettle to on and wrote a sign. One word: BEREAVEMENT, in thick letters. His pen felt heavy. He wanted to Skype Danny's friend in New Zealand but he didn't have a clue as to how. Sure wasn't in the right state of mind to work it out.

Later, when he felt more able, he walked along the promenade. The sea was churning, like his own stomach. It swept in and swept away again, he watched the froth and heard the pebbles. He didn't know where he was going. He didn't really care, he was compelled, one foot in front of the other.

He came to a stop at the pier and bought some tokens for the next bumper car ride. He waited, he cried. In all the years he'd been living here he'd never been on one. The buzzer goes and it's time for his ride. He gets in, gives the token and waits to start. When it crackles into life, he drives his car into a parked one. Tears streaming down his face, he bangs away as other cars avoid him. The empty car drifts into the middle and is hit by others. Jim drives over to another empty one and starts bumping, banging away at that. He doesn't even know he's doing it.

Eventually he's asked by a teenage operator if he'll leave, never come back, he's been given a life ban. He uses his finger to show Jim in what direction he wants him to go. Secretly the operator wouldn't have minded punching the old cunt for bumping away at unmanned cars and messing up the circuit.

Chapter 11

The Sloanes consoled each other with the fact that maybe it had been some sort of freak accident, because there wasn't a suicide note. They couldn't bear that. It was bad enough that he'd come back with Post Traumatic Stress Disorder.

They'd been told, that in these cases (especially with a diary keeper) that there was usually a note. The conclusion was that maybe he'd passed out from his medication with the pencils stuck up his nose, become light-headed and fallen asleep. No-one really knew.

His parents had seen pencils up there before, he'd always done it, how many times had they told him not to. The Sloanes were desperate, searching for a reason, a meaning, for their youngest child's passing.

Of course Joseph came to the funeral, his hands in his pockets and his heart cold. The way he saw it was that his inheritance had just gone up, doubled in fact. A jackpot day, he'd done the maths. What he needed to do was push his parents for a little more life insurance, maybe even get them to buy a flat for their retirement, so that they'd have more life cover.

What they needed was cover, as much cover as he could get down their throats. If only he could entice them with a bit more product. Neither of them had taken Danny's death well. Dark, swollen eyes, Joseph noticed, he was a salesman, salesmen notice weakness, use it to get in and get on top.

The Januarys stood there in black, the three of them, looking like a family. Why he invited Shirley he doesn't really know. Maybe shock, maybe for moral support or maybe to just help with Luke. She didn't know the Sloanes personally, she knew Jim drank with the father but they'd never met.

Luke had taken Danny's death badly, worse than Jim would have expected. Luke was giving tears from his heart. This was the first sun up and sun down he'd experienced in his short life and he really did care for Danny's grieving parents. He couldn't look at them without welling up. And when Jim smiled gently at him he tried to smile back, really tried but he couldn't manage it, couldn't raise his lip. He felt heavy, he felt like he'd never felt before.

Don't cry, Son, don't cry.

Jim whispered to Luke.

They watched the coffin lowered, listened to the wind in the leaves. There was no sanctuary here. The three standing together, Luke crying and Shirley's eyes closed in respect, Jim alone with thoughts of the waste of it all. God knows what the Sloanes must be going through.

He didn't know he was holding his estranged wife's hand as he walked out of the churchyard, through the gate. On realising, he removed it, stopped, looked at Shirley.

I'm sorry, Jim.

She could see the hurt, feel it in his shaking hand. She didn't have time to say anything more before Danny's elder brother, Joseph came up. He was doing the rounds. Shouldering the sad occasion, doing what his parents couldn't do. They were weeping by a hawthorn tree, side by side and no-one dared approach. They weren't up to meeting and greeting. So they left that to their son.

Thanks for coming.

He looks at Jim, then Shirley, he's surprised to see her, he really hadn't thought about her in years, not in years. He feels shocked, it's not so much her face that he recognises, it's her voice, the voice from his very first day at school, the past.

Miss Petticoat?

Yes.

Shirley's taken aback.

You were my teacher, back in primary school, years ago.

Really? I'm sorry, I've taught so many.

Shirley says, not remembering Joseph, how could she? She must have taught hundreds. How could she be expected to remember all the names and faces? They would have changed much more than her. How many had she set on their way, given a gentle push to start on their lives, their journeys?

Joseph remembers her alright, remembers his very first terrifying day and the teacher who now stands before him. She used to take delight in bending over him and whispering into his ear how useless he was. He remembers it happening from that first day. She'd tell him how utterly worthless he was. What had he done? What could he have done to deserve that?

She'd dragged out the agony for a year and spelt the special word daily. He remembers it as if it was yesterday.

Joseph's shaking now, an inner rage and it's not because of his brother.

IDIOT, do you hear me child?

She'd say. Other pupils thought he was a teacher's pet. It looked like it, what with her leaning over, whispering in his ear, smiling and patting his head as she spelt it out: IDIOT child.

Well, I hope I wasn't too strict or too boring. Let me see, how old are you now? Do you remember the year you started school?

She's just talking now, not really knowing what she's saying, just trying to make conversation with a bereaved brother, a brother who is looking ashen, sick.

It's hard to describe how I feel about you.

Oh and why's that?

Shirley's shocked by Joseph's unconcealed anger but he doesn't answer. He turns abruptly and goes to talk to other mourners, all out for the sorrowful day.

He stops by parents of a large middle-aged man with Down's Syndrome who's wearing an Oxford University hoody. They hadn't helped him to blend in much. Jim wondered what kind of person would dress him in something like that. Luke had spotted him during the service, as had others. He'd used him to stare at so he could block out Danny's coffin.

Shirley was genuinely shocked by Joseph's remark.

Why on earth do you think he said that?

I don't know, grief can make people say silly things, I guess.

Jim knows all about that. He'd made the same mistake earlier when he got talking to a couple and mentioned that he'd been barred from the bumper cars for life.

Jim gets his black tie out at least three times a year, sometimes more if it's an unlucky year. He's surprised he's not better at it, made progress in his mourning and mutterings. He even gets a nod from the local vicar now. What with him being such a regular. He once asked Jim if he was a Bush Baptist.

Jim said that indeed he wasn't, he had no idea what one was. He looked it up when he got home - a man of dubious religious conviction - is what he discovered. The vicar was no fool, he'd noticed how Jim never closed his eyes in prayer or put his hands together. They'd had a smile and a one wave relationship ever since. But at least now Jim knew what a Bush Baptist was, because he sure didn't think he'd learnt anything else from the priest, vicar, whatever he was.

He never puts his black tie and suit far away, definitely not in the loft. He'd worry that the moths would get it and he'd have to buy another. That he'll pull it out one day, riddled with holes. He wears if for his regulars, the ones who won't be coming back. A regular is worth at least a hundred quid a year, more, if they take a product or two off the shelf. Three deaths a year and the till took a dent.

What surprised Jim most was that anyone would know his wife's maiden name. He hadn't used it in years, near as damn forgotten that Miss Petticoat had ever existed.

What's with the Miss Petticoat, then? I thought you took January, you sure moaned about it long enough.

Shirley looks at Jim.

I've always used it in class, I thought it sounded softer, safer for the kids, more approachable, if you really want to know.

It's a revelation. He can't remember when he last saw a bit of post drop through the letter box with that name written on it.

So you teach under Petticoat?

I always have. If you'd ever been bothered about my working life, you'd have known that.

So January wasn't ever good enough for you, eh? There's no surprise there.

Jim sounds childish, he hadn't meant to, he's surprised, not hurt.

No, that isn't what I'm saying.

And as was the case for many years now, they left on a

misunderstanding. She wasn't going to explain herself here at a funeral or anywhere else for that matter. Explaining to each other was over.

Luke looks at his parents, shakes his head. If there was one thing Luke knew for certain, one thing life had already taught him at this young age, it was that his parents were total wankers. How they'd ever had a ceasefire long enough to make him he'd never know. He'd always thought one of them must have been gagged. When he thinks of his parents having sex, his eyes roll. He sometimes hopes he was just plopped out of a test tube by a white-coated man with acne. Reckons that could be the reason for his spots. He'd like to ask his parents, but knows enough about them to know that now wouldn't be the best time for asking.

Chapter 12

The thing Shirley noticed about her son when he was born were his feet. What lovely feet and toes he had. She's remembering this as she watches Luke in goal, bouncing up and down, waiting for the ball to come in, trying to keep warm. She's surprised he's in the team, any team really. He hasn't got what is commonly known as coordination, walking has always been a problem and getting up harder.

She's a lone figure on one side of the pitch. Jim's on the other side with the other mums and dads who go every week.

They're a gaggle, Shirley thinks, feeling a little excluded, she'd noted that Jim hadn't even waved.

The team have made it to the semi-finals, a victory will put them into the final. Put them into the local paper.

Shirley hardly ever went, she hated foul weather, hated not having a lie in at the weekend, hated that she hadn't quite come to grips with the offside rule. Above all, she hated the fact it seemed to take up so much of the space between men's ears.

She's always wondered what it would have been like if she'd had a daughter, how different life would have been, all these years later and she still thinks like that. She shakes her head to that thought and looks over to Jim, sees him smiling at a woman who seems to be on her own.

I wonder, Shirley thinks, I wonder if he has. Shirley's still bedding the energetic geriatric.

The ball comes in, Luke jumps, his feet go up into the air. Not only does he have to jump, he has to make a clenched fist and try to punch a moving ball or catch it. That's a lot of coordination, it's all too much. He misses and connects with a boy's face, who's jumping to head it at the same time, knocks him clean out with one punch. Sparko, he's a goner, his legs buckle, he collapses hitting the sodden floor. Jim and other parents invade the pitch to break up the fight that has already started. Boys kicking each other, pushing and pulling, one boy is biting another's leg as one would a lamb chop.

Luke has risen to hero status, his teammates are smiling, patting him around the buttocks as they can't get to his back, guarding him from the onslaught. He's just KO'd the best player on the pitch.

This is exactly why Shirley doesn't come, for scenes like this, to watch a parent and kid rabble. She reads about it in papers, sees it on TV, what attraction football holds she'll never know. If you wanted her honest opinion, she thought the world would be a better place without it.

Luke is shown the red card and asked to leave the pitch, it's held high above the referee's head. He walks off with his hands held in the air like a surrendering prisoner of war, he's shaking his head, he can't bloody well believe it.

I didn't see him ref, honest.

He repeats over and over again.

I was trying to punch the ball, ref.

It didn't help, he's off. Gone.

Awesome.

He hears his number 3 say and it's music to his young ears. He now raises his hands again, not in surrender this time, but in defiant joy. One punch and he's become someone, he sees his mum and smiles, she doesn't respond. He doesn't care. He'd like to mouth - fuck you, Mum - but wouldn't dare.

The other manager's son is carried off between shoulders, bewildered, confused, his red boots bouncing off the grass as if he's been shot among the poppies at Flanders. Shirley recognises the slaughtered boy, she used to teach him, terrible temper, temper like his hair. A temper she'd found hard to control, she isn't as sad as she should be that he's just been punched in the face, knocked clean out.

Luke has just nullified the other team. Ginger's dad gives up ten hours of his life a week to run and manage them so his son could have finals, win cups, show his undoubted talents and maybe get a contract. Not so some gormless goalie can knock him clean out. He's livid and goes berserk, shaking the ref for extra time when the final whistle blows. Shaking him like a man would a piggy bank looking for his last pound. He doesn't realise it, but he's just got himself a season long touchline ban. Longer, if the ref beefs up the evidence, which he will. He'll be banned from having any future involvement with the training of kids. This ref's not going to be manhandled on a wet Sunday morning for a tenner. By Monday a report will be in the post and the coach will be struck off, banned, put on a black list, never to coach again. Not in this country anyway. The ref's heard of stories, ref-rumours that families have uprooted to live in Spain, just so ill-tempered dads can watch their sons play football and beat up the next ref. There's many ref bashers doing time in Spain. It's a reason he'd never go there, never. No, Greece is where he takes his well-earned rest, he can't believe how cheap it is at the moment. He's told friends to take their hard earned pounds there.

Jim has his arm around his dirty-legged giraffe of a son,

congratulating him on reaching the final. Not the punch, though, which Luke secretly thinks clinched the win.

Luke had been low since Danny's death, more withdrawn, if that could be possible, it was. Jim hasn't told Shirley, she'd only make a fuss. Use some psycho babble, some teacher crap, something Jim wouldn't really understand or be able to argue with, so he kept his worries quiet and watched out for his son.

Shirley's walking behind them, listening to the after match man talk, as they head to their separate cars. She's not sure why she came, her son doesn't seem bothered and she knows for sure her ex-husband isn't interested in seeing her. He's hardly looked at her or said a word. She seems to be the one who instigates any type of conversation, wonders if it was always the case.

Jim sees the ginger kid.

Did you say sorry or shake his hand?

No!

I think you should, go on.

Luke looks at his dad, then his mum.

That's so retarded, Dad.

What do you mean, retarded?

Stupid. He means stupid, Jim.

Shirley says, interpreting.

I know what bloody retarded means.

Jim says, jerking his head around, reacting angrily. The truth was that Luke was worried about the other kid's dad. He'd already called him a prick, when he'd come running. It's not every day Luke got called a prick by a grown up, figured he'd better keep a distance.

Just do it.

Jim says, annoyed. Luke walks away, sulking, with his hands in his shorts, his head hung low, he's way too big not to be noticed. He looks pathetic.

Shirley lets him take a few steps and says loudly:

Luke. Don't. Come back here.

Luke stops, he can't believe it. He's always thought his mum was stricter than his dad, a bit mad actually. He's much more wary of her temper, she's slapped him more than once. He stops.

That's great, what an example. What sort of teacher are you?

Look, Jim, do we need to have an argument about

absolutely everything? Especially here in front of everyone. Is that what you want?

She says making a wide gesture with her hands.

Actually, yes we do. You tell me what's wrong with him walking over there and saying sorry, shaking the kid's hand. Like any normal person would.

The kid's a prick.

I've heard it all now, Jesus Christ, the kid's a prick, fucking hell.

Jim's never heard her talk about another child like that. She'd called Jim one plenty of times, but she's never used it about a kid. He'd like to laugh, but Luke's watching, expecting some sort of reaction.

You've done some changing, that's all I can say. Well there you go, Son, don't bother. It's come from your own mother's foul mouth. He's a prick, Ginger's a prick. Fuck me! You've changed, love. You should be well and truly proud of yourself.

Drop the love bit.

Shirley says keeping her composure.

All Luke hopes is that Ginger's dad hasn't heard what his son's just been called, the part about being a prick.

He's never thought of his dad as hard, couldn't see his words being backed up with a punch.

So, I don't have to say sorry, then?

Luke asks, running past his dad, wanting to reach the safety of the car and it's locks before it got nasty.

No, you heard what your mum said, he's a prick. See you love.

Jim says, getting an annoying last jab in as Luke makes for the cover of the car.

And they drive away, Luke and Jim in one car, Shirley in another.

Luke looks at his dad's hands gripping the wheel, sees the whites of the knuckles and says, trying to change the ambience:

I think you're right, Mum's changed.

Changed? She's fucking unbelievable.

Jim says.

Chapter 13

Giving away the dream had brought it back to life. The bike sat there in the darkness, like it always had, but it wasn't the same anymore, it was unsettling Jim. It was a reminder of Danny's last night on earth. The map's the same, he can't look at it anymore. He'd come close to ripping it down or at the very least rolling it up, he'd done neither, because it hides mould on the wall behind it.

The trouble with Jim and he knows it, knows it like winter follows summer, is that he's not an adventurous man. Worse than that, thinks maybe he's a bit of a coward. Jim January might have had the odd *National Geographic* knocking around the house, in the barbers, but at best, he was an armchair traveller. Dreams versus fear, fear won every time, hadn't it always, hadn't it as a child? Maybe that's why the *National Geographic*'s got a yellow spine. Yellow for all the people who won't dare. Yellow for the scared, yellow for the yellow belly, yellow for people like me. He despises himself, he doesn't want to be that type of man anymore. He's had enough of being him, he's so bored of himself.

He hopes his son will be fine, he's at a strange age, Jim hardly breaks through anymore, he tries, but his son's lost in that hinterland, between child and man, covered in the permafrost called adolescence. Even if Jim used a drill he doesn't think he would break through.

He knows that the barbers will be okay. He owns it, no debt. It wouldn't matter if he put others behind the chair and picked up rent or not. It didn't matter, nothing mattered, apart from one thing, Jim didn't want to be a coward anymore.

He takes a deep breath, picks up the receiver, no small talk, not a word, knows she'll be on a break, just comes out with it.

I'm thinking of going away, I'm not sure when, but if I do would you look after Luke for me? Well us.

She'd look after Luke, but Shirley wasn't going to let an opportunity like this go:

Don't tell me, let's guess, that bike thingy. So, you're finally going to do it then, what's its name, oh, I remember, the Rocket.

And she laughs. She'd heard it all before. It sickened her.

You can be a right bitch, do you know that? I'm going to try and live a little of my dream.

He says with irritation, regrets it immediately, what on earth is he telling her that for?

Running away more like, that's what you're really doing, Jim. Anyway, in answer to your original question, of course I'll take care of my son.

Jim's already said more than he'd wanted. Truth be told, he didn't have that many people to tell. And then Jim comes up with just the right response.

I think you'll find you did the running away.

Jim's pleased with the punch he got in there, about head height he reckons, a nice punch to end a telephone call with.

Shirley had no idea why she'd acted in the way she had. Didn't she care what Jim did? She really didn't. It was happening more and more. It was as if she was in self-destruct mode. Her mask was slipping and what lay behind was starting to show.

She'd been lucky to get away with a wayward comment to a parent when she'd said:

What your child needs is a sliver of hope and I don't see you capable of giving that.

The parent hadn't heard, she was too busy mentally digesting last night's EastEnders. She'd already phoned a friend to talk about it on the walk to school. She can't wait to partake in another dollop. What she loved about it was the flight of fantasy away from her own dull life.

Luke was walking past the barbers when he saw his dad sitting in the chair, staring into space. He taps on the window, his dad doesn't respond, doesn't smile, doesn't move, doesn't do a damn thing.

He's so weird, Luke thinks, walks on and then turns back, decides to have another look. Jim's still sitting there. Hasn't moved, hasn't blinked, he's a shop dummy, Luke thinks. He opens the door.

Dad?

He says, going in, already regretting that he's there. His school blazer splattered with the spillages of the year. His feet point to Jim, like big Malibu boards, the ones old Hawaiians surf big waves on.

Luke?

Jim says in a soft voice. A voice his son doesn't recognise. And then Jim breaks down. He hadn't meant to, hadn't planned it, hadn't waited for his son to come in (he never normally did). He'd already missed out on three punters while he'd been sitting, staring into space.

Luke doesn't know what to do. So he stands in the middle of the room with his hands by his sides, like a tin solider.

He takes a step, then another with his Malibu feet and slowly comes over to the chair, he leans forward and touches his dad, a gentle touch. His size casts a shadow over Jim.

You know what, Son? I've been sitting here thinking that I might be a coward.

They're looking at each other in the mirror. Same nose, same ears, same eyes.

Oh.

Luke says without conviction, as he does most things. But he knows one thing, he doesn't want his dad to be that.

I think I might be, Son. I really think I might be.

Luke's not seen his dad like this. In fact he'd never seen any adult like this and he doesn't like it, sure doesn't know how to respond. Adults know things or at least make out they do and they definitely don't cry and that's just the way Luke likes it.

Why? What've you done?

It's what I've not done. It's the bike, the Rocket, because of the trip I never took, the one I was trying to push onto Danny. I was being a coward.

Oh God, not that word again, Luke thinks.

It's the most revealing thing Jim's ever said about himself, he looks at Luke and wipes away a small tear. He's not had many of these father to son moments, this might well be the first. Luke's not liking it and he's sure not going to say anything.

Having a bike in the garage and a map on a wall isn't enough. In the end it all comes down to doing things.

Jim wants to pass onto his son what he himself hasn't got, the big C: confidence. Or at least a decent set of balls.

Luke thinks this is odd.

I've got to do it, Son, otherwise, I'm all pants and no trousers.

Where does that saying come from? Jim thinks, after saying it.

You're well sad, Dad.

Is all Luke can muster up. He's using other people's language, hiding behind it like a wall. He doesn't really want to say that. He sure doesn't want to see his dad cry. He doesn't know what to say or how to act. One thing above all else, he doesn't want anyone he knows to walk by.

I want to be a good example. Do you understand what I'm saying?

Luke looks at his dad, tries to smile and says:

I think so.

He hoped the atmosphere would change.

What I'm trying to say, in a round about sort of way, is I'm thinking of going away for a bit, travelling, doing the bike trip I should have done years ago. Would you be alright staying with your mum while I'm away?

He'd finally got it out. Now he really must go and do it or he'd forever be held up as a coward in his son's eyes. He wouldn't want that.

Do it then, I don't care, why don't you fuck off right now?

Luke's upset, angry, surprised. His dad's gone and done it again, ambushed him. Luke wants all this stuff, this mum and dad stuff to stop, all these surprises to stop, he's fed up with their pathetic surprises.

So what you waiting for? Just do it, go on, I don't care.

Luke's trembling, angry, sure doesn't want to stay with his lunatic of a mum.

If it wasn't for your education you could come. I'd love to take you. If I get the hang of it, maybe we could go together when you're a bit older?

What Jim doesn't know, what no-one knows is educationally Luke is sinking. Education to Luke is like being stuck on an island as the rest of the class walk down to the jetty, slowly board the boat and pull away. But at least the dream of being fed and fucked by penguins has stopped. Luke looks at his dad, he hadn't realised he was sitting in his lap like the child he is. He gets up, backs away, embarrassed. He doesn't like his dad crying and he's sick of this coward shit. Mostly he wished he hadn't knocked on the window and come in. None of this would be happening if he hadn't. Luke mumbles something and is out the door before Jim even notices.

He'd been lost in thought for a moment, about the state of his body. Every time he bends over he thinks that maybe he won't be able to get back up. He makes a creaking noise going down, sighing noise coming up. Age was creeping in and over him like a vine taking over a derelict house. Eyes first, then stiffness in the morning and a new ache before he goes to sleep. The thing is, Jim's getting old and he bloody well knows it.

Chapter 14

Rules, it's all about rules and sticking to them.

If you said you were going to do something, you did it. She hated indecision, not taking action, that was Jim's bloody way, not hers.

Shirley didn't bluff, never let a child call her by her first name. It was unprofessional, a distance is what it took, to maintain control and teach in a professional manner, to extract the best and most out of a child. She kept it that way, she had boundaries, didn't make exceptions and expected to be called Miss Petticoat at all times, it might be old-fashioned but it was the way she liked it.

Shirley has just excluded a troublesome child, his brother had been the same and judging by the bump, the hump, coming out of the mother, there's another one on its way. That'll be the same, illiterate and time consuming.

She keeps these thoughts tucked under her bob, colleagues don't know. She walks the troublesome child out of the class and tells him to wait outside the door until she calls him back in.

I'll let you know when.

She says softly, turning to go back to her class. He's six, he's been excluded three times already this week, spent nearly as long outside as in. Shirley doesn't care. He takes up a lot of her attention and time, time which could best be spent on other kids, children that want and are trying to learn. His type could stand in the corridor, kicking the wall, the door, for as long as he likes, because every time he does she adds an extra minute. She didn't get involved in a power struggle with children. She was in control, she told them what was what.

Her method of teaching has changed over the years and she knows the exact day, minute, month and year, when she, Miss Petticoat, could truly say she was no longer a believer in the system.

The bell had gone and she had called the children back from lunch. One boy was missing, he usually was. She'd given up lunch breaks, come in with new ideas, tried to make learning fun, tried to find a way that worked best for him personally, nothing had.

This was before CCTV doors and gates, hysteria and neon flak jackets, long before all that false sense of security.

Shirley was asked to find him, she'd wished ever since that she hadn't. It hadn't surprised her that Derek was missing. Nothing had changed, all the education, time and money, he'd stayed the same. She'd put in hours, tried, she really had, tried more than most. This had been back when she'd been full of ideas and doctrines, willing to give everything a go, before her shutters had come down.

Shirley had walked around, checking toilets and then she'd found him. He was lying on top of a girl, burning her dark hair with a lighter. The girl was trying to beat him off. The young teacher really had thought that the frightened girl would go up in flames in front of her, at the very least lose all her hair.

The attack made the local and national papers. Miss Petticoat was interviewed, externally (by the papers) and internally (by the school). A little of her had died that very day. They'd seemed more interested in the boy than the girl. She'd been questioned about whether more could have been done for the child, wanted to find the answer to what had created such a little monster, perhaps he was a victim as well. Miss Petticoat's conclusion was that it wasn't hers or any other teacher's fault. He was rotten before he'd got there, rotten before he ever got to school, rotten as soon as he'd dropped from the womb. Derek could have been given all the one to one education society could afford and still it wouldn't have been enough. All the time and money wasted. Shirley had come to the conclusion that you couldn't give Derek what he wasn't first shown at home. Interest, love and above all, hope. As far as she was concerned if you didn't come from a home with those ingredients or at least one of them, you wouldn't rise. It didn't matter what a teacher did or didn't do, the chances were that the child was already turning rotten, like an apple at the bottom of a dark barrel.

Sophie Townsend had never come back. The family moved her to another school. Traumatised for life, Shirley had thought, put all the counselling you wanted in place and you'd still have a ruined girl. She pitied her, pitied the family and vowed never to let it happen again. Not on her watch, never, she'd watch out for other little Dereks in the making.

As for Derek, he went into special measures and had a fortune spent on him. Before his fourteenth birthday, he was sleeping behind bars in a young offender's home, apparently he'd even set fire to that. The last Shirley had heard, he'd attacked a visiting French student and doused her in petrol for talking French.

Shirley had read about it in the local paper. There was always some character in it that she knew. She remembers reading it in the staff room as she crunched on a few mints.

Nothing worked for children like him. She was absolutely cast-iron certain of that. If anyone had asked and she'd been allowed to be frank, honest, open, hadn't worried about losing her job, her career, her pension, making enough to meet the mortgage and car payments. If she could have been honest, spoken freely, she would have said and she should know, because if she didn't, who would? She had spent over a quarter of a century on the front line, more than others got for murder. She'd say she knew what kind of child he was, had known it as soon as he walked in through her classroom door. The way he interacted with others, she had known. From that moment, the moment she'd come round the corner and seen him on top of the girl with a lighter in his hand, she'd vowed to protect the Sophies, she no longer cared about the Dereks of this world. She'd kept that hush hush, though, had never let those types of thoughts out.

She'd learnt that isolation worked and used it more and more (hence the crying boy outside, kicking the door). He'd be allowed in when he quietened.

She no longer believed in the 'no child left behind' mantra, didn't believe in it at all. She'd decide who was worth saving and who was going to the wall.

No-one knew this, not even Jim. She'd still tick the ever increasing boxes, make all the right mutterings, nod her head in all the right places in front of the young head, a modern educationalist, willing to embrace all the new and latest ideas passed from above to below. No-one could be left in any doubt how she embraced them. Shirley would nod her head and say yes and ask good questions.

Of course kids failed. What annoyed Shirley most was all this lightweight, lib-lab, half baked natter from above. How many years had the theorists spent on the front line in a classroom?

The 'saving one and all' theory, as far as Miss Petticoat was concerned, was wasted natter from the educationalists above. It made no difference to the Dereks of the world, none whatsoever. There'd always be one hatching after him and one after that. A conveyor belt of dross.

Chapter 15

Jim buffed and shined as the weather got warmer, the sun brighter. He opened the garage door and brought the bike from the dark to the blue sky, sang 'Rocket Man', but couldn't remember all of Elton's lines.

Since he made his tearful decision, he's no longer afraid. A weight had been lifted, he'd been reborn, in his forty-ninth year he'd come alive, he wanted to make the most of what time he had left. He put his helmet on and rode the five hundred metres it took to get to the mechanics. He'd done shorter rides. He was going to have the brake cable changed by a father and son team. A thing he'd discovered about them and he'd had to discover it (they weren't big talkers) was that, the father and son mechanical team would only date mothers and daughters, kept it in the family, so to speak.

Found any more combos?

Jim asked, taking off his helmet. He said it, not because he was interested but because he had absolutely nothing else to say. He liked them, but they weren't really conversationalists. They'd known each other for over twenty years and small talk was not their thing.

For people who didn't like talking, they sure seemed to have a strange hobby, Jim had always thought.

Alright to pick it up later?

Sure, so where you going this year?

It had been a standing joke with the mechanics, how the mileage from one MOT to the next never really went up, hardly moved at all. They had lots of clients like Jim, who had machines they never used. Shiners is what the father and son called them. Jim's a shiner.

I might surprise you.

They didn't think he would. This was quite a conversation, more than they'd had in years. Feeling liberated, Jim asks:

So, when are you going to let me at your hair?

He'd always wanted to cut it and now seemed the right time to ask.

I always like to keep business and pleasure separate, if you don't mind.

For them it was simple, business was business and pleasure was pleasure if they could find the right mother and daughter team.

They had the best kept heads in town, good haircuts, but hair never cut by Jim. He didn't like that, didn't like the fact that they went up the coast to have it done. They'd been spotted, news like that travels in a small town. Jim wondered why he wasn't good enough. If they were fine for his bike why wasn't he good enough for their hair?

I'll get you one day, even if I have to get you in your sleep.

Jim says, before waving his byes. The father and son didn't respond. Jim knew that he probably never would, he couldn't see those two ever coming through his door. The garage could be seen reflected in his mirrors. He'd watched the son grow from a kid to a man. Sometimes, Jim wished they weren't so convenient, so that he could take his business elsewhere.

Jim's got a head he's trying to finish up on, grey hair falling to the floor. He doesn't like talking on the phone in public spaces, he's old-fashioned enough to find it rude. He doesn't like it when customers come in talking on their mobiles as if he's not there. He'd only taken the call because Charlie's name popped up, registered. He wouldn't have picked up for anyone else, hadn't heard from him since Danny's funeral. Jim thought he would need space, time to recover. In fact it's a little more than that, Jim didn't exactly know what to say. So he'd decided on no action, not saying a word, as being the best course to take. He regretted that now, hearing his haunted voice. Jim couldn't bear to think how bad it must be for a father to lose a son.

He'd had a dream soon after Danny died, a carnival float passed by with all the dead he'd ever known on it, friends, family and Danny. A flotilla of dead wavers, waving at Jim.

Hello Jim, Charlie here. We've been going through Danny's diaries and I thought you'd like to know you're in them.

Jim doesn't know what to say, hadn't at the funeral, doesn't now, so he remains silent, waits for his friend to say something else, hopes he will.

Jim's noticed straight away that Charlie's done away with the small talk, done away with any trace of it at all. Usually he was a titbit man.

He's written some nice things, I'm really just ringing to thank you for trying to teach and help him. I've been going through them, reading and whatnot. He's got everything written down, you'd be surprised, loads of detail.

Jim can't stay silent; he's got to say what's been on his mind.

Charlie, there's a lot of ways to say sorry and I know saying sorry will never be enough, but I'll say it anyway, I'm so sorry Charlie.

He's glad to have said it because it's been on his mind ever since Danny died and all the months that have passed. At the funeral, all he'd managed to do was shake his hand and nod and to make sure he didn't make eye contact.

I'm glad I've got them, I really am. To tell you the truth they're a comfort.

Charlie says, his voice goes down a notch.

Jim's hoping, praying his friend isn't going to cry. If he cries, Jim thinks, I'm a goner.

I'm trying to make contact with the people in them, don't ask me why. Just thought you'd like to know. To tell you the truth, I can't go forward so I'm going back in time. Is that strange?

It's a question he wants an answer to.

No, not at all, I guess you grab at whatever you've got left.

Jim regrets using the word grab immediately.

I'm grabbing alright. Bye for now, Jim.

As quickly as his voice came, it's gone. Jim worries whether he could have been more tactful, knowing he shouldn't have used the word grabbed.

He goes back to the cut with sadness running through his hand onto the snipping, cold steel blades. The customer has no idea how lucky he was for his hair to have turned grey (he'd done nothing but moan about it since it had).

Chapter 16

Charlie had used the key to get to his son's diaries and start reading. He'd spread them all over his bedroom floor and got them into their year order. He'd been glad that his wife had been so consistent at buying them. He hadn't bought a single one, not that it had mattered when Danny was alive, it did now. Like the sports days he'd missed and the waving off at the station as his son went off to war. Too busy working, too busy being busy. And for what?

The thing Charlie can't figure out is why the last three weeks were missing, torn from the diary. It's a clue, but to what? He'll find out, if he, Charlie, could chase back through looms to a wiring fault he's sure he'll find the reason to the missing pages.

He reads the diaries in secret and his wife is making a quilt out of her dead son's clothes. Neither know what the other is up to. She hopes to sleep under it before next winter. That's with or without her husband's approval. She'd taken to waking at night, cutting cloth and sewing under a light then spends most of the day in bed in a stupor. Charlie thinks it's depression but he doesn't know how to talk to her or heal her or do anything to help.

Chapter 17

The next call came in on the landline, so Jim had no problems taking it behind his beads. It was a secretary from Luke's school who wanted Jim to explain his son's repeated absences, sixteen mornings already that term. He couldn't.

Well I think you need to come in as soon as possible for a chat.

Jim didn't know how to react to the news. A part of him was just happy his son was alive. Considering the other phone call he'd taken earlier. It could have been worse, much much worse. He had to keep things in perspective here. Maybe it was his and Shirley's fault? Maybe he's been too soft, not focused enough. Maybe too hard (he makes Luke take his plates to the dishwasher). He can't load it, it's too complicated. One thing Jim knows for sure, is that he's going to get himself up to the school sharpish.

Jim picked up his bike, didn't bother with any small talk

this time. He knew it wouldn't matter to them, wouldn't seem rude. Machinery and monkey wrenches, mothers and daughters were their thing.

He rode up the hill, where there's a good view of the town, along to Luke's school. His brake cable feels good, firm in his hand, he starts singing 'Take Me Home Country Road' and he's dancing and singing on his seat, he doesn't know why. It could be the weather, the longer nights, the sky turning from grey to blue.

Jim had never liked school or authority, he hadn't done very well himself. He drops a gear and slings his motorbike into a corner, it feels good, opens it up along a straight, he might be middle aged, but at this precise moment he feels very young and alive.

He arrives at his destination and is met by a large (well if Jim's brutally honest, obese) woman. Jim has no idea how hard she fights, it's a constant battle and she'd been losing it all her life. A life of losing, lost in primary school, lost in secondary, losing since she joined the work force. Now she's given up giving up, her housebound husband likes her just the way she is, bobble and wobble with diabetes waiting at the end of the path.

Jim follows her, swishing, swaying, down a corridor smelling of disinfectant, bucket and brushes. She passes him into the efficient hands of the Education Welfare Officer.

Follow me, please.

She's abrupt, been bossy all her life, it's one of the reasons she goes for jobs like this, the power. When they get to her office she asks Jim to sit down as she closes the door. She's all matter of fact and getting on with it. It's all an act really.

As you can see.

She says, leaning over, tapping the register. Jim can't believe they still use them, haven't moved on. She shows him all the missing ticks next to Luke's name.

As you can see, his attendance is sporadic at best. Are there any health issues we need to be aware of?

It was more than obvious Luke hadn't been going, hardly at all. What was it with people who worked with children? He wasn't listening anymore. He was wondering why teachers always have to talk to adults as if they're children as well. Must be the environment.

Sorry, who did you say you were, again? Jim says.

I'm the EWO, Education Welfare Officer.

A wastrel officer, you're joking?

Jim really did think that's what she'd said. That some Government bureau, some fresh out of college idiot, has come up with this good old-fashioned word, instead of bunker, truant or twagger.

No, no, a Welfare Officer, not wastrel officer.

She says, smiling.

I'm sorry, do you wear a star? Are you the married?

Jim asks, trying to be funny. It comes out wrong. He'd meant to say marshal, instead of married. He's nervous. He'd wanted to take the piss out of the title, like she's a sheriff or something. He thought that if he could make her laugh, then perhaps she'd go easy on his son.

I don't think that's any of your business, Mr January.

She says, sucking in her stomach, looking into Jim's eyes.

I was married, not now, we're separated, she's a teacher, like yourself.

Jim says, trying to get the conversation back onto an even keel, but what he's actually doing is digging, digging a big hole.

The officer could get to like a man who thought she was a teacher, which she wasn't, she was an EWO, but the man in front of her didn't need to know that.

The most interesting thing about her own husband, who'd be sitting waiting for his dinner at home, is that he'd named their house Casa after going to Spain. The thing he doesn't know is his wife added nova at the end. She had to laugh, she'd not seen an erection in years. He was as far removed from a Casanova as you could get. For him taking the bins out was a heart pumping adventure. Easy is what he wanted out of life, easy was how he lived it. How she got lumbered with husband number two she couldn't work out, there must have been a spark once. She wouldn't hesitate to jump ship if the right man came along. Hers didn't do birthday cards, Christmas, forget Valentine's, he couldn't see the point, couldn't see the point in anything apart from a TV screen or his fish tank.

I'm sorry to hear that you've split up from your wife.

Maybe he really is making a play for me she thinks, studying his eyes, running hers down his thighs. Jim looks at the lady, he can't remember her name.

Maybe it's our fault. Me and my ex's that is. You know, why Luke's bunking.

Jim gets up to leave, he doesn't know what else to say. He doesn't want to make any more mistakes.

Oh, I doubt that. I don't see why that should be the case at all. Take one of these.

The officer says getting to her feet with a leaflet in her hand.

It's our eight point plan. It might be of some help. Any problems don't hesitate to call. Here's my card.

Thanks.

Jim says, taking it from her hand.

Any problems and I mean anything, just ring that number.

And ever so slightly she pushes out her breasts, feels the fabric straining. She'd never met a man who didn't like them, didn't want to put their hands all over them given half a chance.

Chapter 18

The split had hurt Luke. Not his parents being apart, that was easy. No, what hurt Luke was the fact that he didn't have a clue what was happening until it was upon him. Everything was one big surprise. As far as he was concerned, looking back, he'd only been sent on a holiday so they could split. They'd lied, the best phrase he could come up with was that his parents had been, well sneaky.

And now he's got to listen to his dad going on about not going to school. He'd got away with it for so long by sending the early morning texts from his dad's mobile.

Honestly, Dad, I can't remember, it's not important, it's all so boring, what's it matter if I go to school or not, you didn't?

He's starting talking to his dad as an equal. Jim's not so sure he likes being his equal. Not sure about all the swearing and not sure what he should do.

What do you mean it's not important? Of course it's important.

Jim's trying to get to the bottom of it without losing his rag. He doesn't want to tell Shirley.

I'll tell you this, if your mum finds out, it's adios amigo.

Luke laughs, he's on the puff, he's funny and bored in equal measures now. Secretly he's been selling his mum's clothes, shoes and such on ebay to finance it. He sure can't be bothered to get a proper job. Slowly he's been clearing out the loft and once he's finished with his mum's he'll start on his dad's. He's quite the entrepreneur, getting lots of positive feedback, unbelievably the merchandise is packed and posted the same day and his dad hasn't noticed a thing.

Shirley knew Luke wasn't going to school, she's not a fool, she knows the system, the rules, how to make them and break them. The officer had, in fact, rung her before Jim. Shirley was the first name on the emergency contact list. She'd made sure of that. She knew the procedure, knew what was what.

She'd been left an urgent message but was mid-lesson and when she'd finally had the time, it had already been arranged that Jim would visit, or as the officer had said.

He's actually on his way.

She'd thought about turning up at the same time but she knew it would create a scene and wanted what was best for her son, this wasn't about them.

Shirley's at home with a tuna and sweetcorn sandwich on a plate, waiting for Jim and his call.

He'd better not sweep this under the carpet, like he sweeps his hair, his day, his life, she thinks.

Luke's not bothered, he's not saying much, he doesn't even know what the problem is. He's got caught, so what?

Fuck it, he thinks, he might become an entrepreneur, lots of them were crap at school.

Get over it, Dad. What's the worst thing that can happen to me? I've already been caught.

He's right, Jim thinks, what can I do?

Look, all I know is you've been missing most of your mornings. Is everything alright, are you okay? This isn't about me and your mum, is it?

Jim knows it's a leading question, shouldn't have said it. He'd listened to his wife for years to know that.

Yeah, I'm well fed up being caught in your war, caught in the crossfire, getting hit by shrapnel. It sucks, you know what? I just want to be left alone.

Luke all of a sudden looks his age, fourteen and ten months. It saddens Jim that Luke has had to witness all the mess and residue of their dead relationship, wishes he, they, could be more mature about it, but they're not. Deep down, Luke doesn't give a toss.

Well if you could talk to me occasionally that would be a start, little words, then move on to sentences when you're ready.

Jim's making every effort to keep calm, but he can feel he's getting angry, feels that beat in his heart, the frustration creeping. So he takes a deep breath and breathes in and starts to count to ten. One, two, three. But Luke interrupts him.

If you want my opinion, I think you're both pathetic.

He gives Jim his surly stare and a raise of a lip, he got it about a year ago and uses it most days.

Really, I don't care what you or Mum do. I don't give a toss.

There, said it, he thinks, flicking his hair.

Well, if you don't give a toss, at least tell me what you've been up to, what you've been doing with your time?

Jim hopes he's not spending all this free time in bed. He feels like his own dad, when he used to tell him off, legs apart, arms crossed, frowning.

Luke had never really given them any concerns, not really, he was a good kid, mostly did what he was told. Jim doesn't want to create a scene, doesn't want to say something he might regret, in fact he doesn't know what else to say and Luke knows it. This is an unusual situation for both of them and Jim sure isn't winning. If indeed this is about winning, Jim's not so sure it is. He just wants the lines of communication to remain open, to keep the friendship bunting fluttering.

Luke knows there's no point lying, keeping quiet, his Dad's never really told him off in his life, he's not afraid of him. Now if his mum had been standing opposite that would have been a different story altogether.

I've been going fishing.

Jim's confused.

Fishing? Who with? I never knew you fished.

Jim had never been, not even for mackerel, which got pulled out of the sea four or five to a line. It had never looked like fishing to Jim, never seemed to take the fishermen more than a minute to pull up another brace. Jim has no idea why mackerel cost so much, but he knew that the men who caught them stank. When a mackerel man walked in for a haircut it was like a shoal had swum through the door.

You don't know anything about me, Dad, do you?

Luke says it in a way that means and you never will.

Fishing! Is it any good?

Jim's interested.

It's alright.

At least his son's talking, found an interest in something.

That's good, Jim thinks, could have been a lot worse. He could have been injecting, sniffing, drinking. Jim's relieved.

Who do you go with? I didn't know any of your mates fished?

He realises he doesn't know any of Luke's friends, not any more. They all stopped talking. Even his football mates who used to sing songs together in the car don't now, they're more likely to be fixing hair with pocket mirrors, combing the wax through, preening.

Jim's noticed the young men becoming obsessed with their looks. Who's he to complain, he'll make good money from them, in the future. Well he hopes he will but they'll probably all be heading for a unisex salon, want that extra reassuring touch.

If you really want to know, I went with Danny, before he died. He was teaching me.

That was something Charlie Sloane had read in the diaries that he didn't want to bring up with Jim on the phone. His son could rest in peace, God bless him. He wasn't going to tell him that.

Charlie's been reading and rereading the diaries since Danny's death. He's found out many things a father shouldn't know and other things he should have known while he was alive. He still had some years to travel back through. It was all he did now, reading and rereading, going over the lines, highlighting.

Danny. You went fishing with Danny? When? Why'd you go with that idiot?

Jim's angry, regrets saying idiot as soon as it slides from his mouth.

Look, I shouldn't have said that, that was very unfair of me, forget I said that.

He's trying to correct himself, but he had thought Danny had been a selfish idiot to take away his own life. His death had made Jim angry, angry for himself, angry for Charlie and angry for the brother he'd left, angry that he could have even been partly responsible in some way. Guilty, is what he mainly felt.

Now he's worried that Danny talked about depression or suicide with Luke, what sort of twisted logic, what poison, what pus, he might have put into his young head. He's thinking all this, while staring at his only son, praying to God he doesn't go the same way.

Jim gets it now, it's all making sense, he nods his head to himself. Why Danny had wanted an eleven o'clock start, instead of ten. Why he had two rods and two pairs of boots, why there seemed to be two of everything resting by the wall. The devious bastard, right under my nose, Jim thinks and in a blink of an eye, Danny's memory has been tarnished, trashed.

Jim knew Danny fished, it was one of the things he'd missed most on his tour of Iraq.

The only fishing I did there was in a well and I didn't bring up any fish.

He'd then gone on to tell Jim exactly what he had brought up, it had eyes but it sure wasn't a fish.

Well did you catch anything worth missing an education for?

Jim asks.

He's shocked, annoyed, upset that he's been lied to. No, worse than that, he's been tricked, cheated. He'd given his son more than enough rope (line in Luke's case). Jim hates himself for introducing Danny to his son's impressionable life. Luke doesn't have the time to answer, he's saved by the phone. Saved isn't really the right word. It's Shirley, his mother.

You sound nice, calm and relaxed.

Jim says.

She doesn't, not at all. He hasn't spoken to her for a month, more. He hasn't wanted to and neither has she. Shirley's been having private dancing lessons with her pensioner. She's spending her days with children and nights with an old man.

Do I? I shouldn't.

She'd try her hardest to make sure her son didn't end up like Jim, uneducated and lacking motivation. She wouldn't allow it. Her ex could rest with the little education he had but she wasn't going to allow a son of hers to follow him as an example. She was going to do something about it and she was about to do it right now.

Oh and why's that?

How the hell does she know, what is she, some sort of oracle? Jim thinks.

Come on Jim, what do you take me for, a fool?

He's never thought that, lots of other things but never a fool.

I know the school rang you.

How come she's always one step ahead of the game, like a horse, one fence clear?

Well, if you already know, what do you suggest?

Jim thinks he got a good shot in there, especially seeing as he's under pressure.

Don't make this personal, Jim. This is about what's best for Luke, our son, remember. I won't be drawn into any stupid argument with you or side tracked. That is, if you don't mind, of course.

What is it about teachers and the way they persist in talking? Jim thinks. He wonders what it is about them as a couple that makes them behave like this. Makes them behave like they were down to the bare metal, the rust, everything catching and cutting.

What do you suggest? I'm open to suggestions. I'm all ears.

He is.

Shirley's not, she's already made up her mind. It's obvious, it starts and ends with Luke coming home, well, coming to live with her and getting him away from his incapable, useless, I want to go away on my motorbike, stick a thumb in my mouth, Dad.

The thing is I've only just spoken to Luke. We're getting to the bottom of it, give us some time and we'll figure it out.

Jim tries to be assertive.

Figure it out? You haven't even got any books on your shelves. What's he got to say for himself anyway? Put him on.

What on earth was she thinking when she'd given her son an option? You don't give children options. She should have just told him. Didn't she do it all day in her job? So why on earth had she been so soft on her wayward son? What was she thinking?

Shirley's not asking but telling Jim and he knows it. He puts the phone down on the side and whispers.

Don't tell your mum about Danny. Say you went fishing, say all that but don't tell her about Danny, she'll go mad.

Jim wants to protect Danny from her wrath. One wishing ill of the dead in one day was bad enough. He looks at Luke as he speaks, he's nervous, keeps jiggling, crossing and un-crossing his legs, he's uncomfortable.

Chapter 19

It's decided, Luke's going to Shirley or she's going to court.

It's his choice, Jim knows she would, so it's no choice at all. He also knows she'd win what with her being a teacher, better with words, better at being in front of the world, better at making sense of it all. Jim's more of a bumbler.

Luke was livid, sulky and as he put it himself: really fucked off. He hadn't wanted to go, no bloody way. Said he wouldn't, said he'd run away, said all sorts of things, added he'd never talk to his dad again. Said his dad was nothing but a loser and a coward. Said he'd throw as much shit as he could Jim's way. All Jim had time to say was that it was for the best and then before he knew it, Shirley had knocked at the door and his only son was packed and gone.

He'd stood by the door and watched helplessly as they drove away. His son turned, gave him a finger and then made the wanker sign, mouthed it so Jim was sure.

Well he only had himself to blame, Jim thought, feeling hurt, angry and already lonely.

Luke promised himself that he'd make his mum's life hell, he'd make both of their lives hell and he'd start by not talking, not saying a word, not to either of them. It shouldn't be that hard. In fact he thought he'd be quite good at it, he'd been in training for years.

So far, Luke had been good to his word, not a text, not a phone call. Jim's tried to call him and he knows Luke's always got the thing by his side, it never leaves him, it's like he's a cowboy with his pistol. It's his comforter, his dummy, his link with the outside world. He'd lost it once and thrown a tantrum; when Jim had offered him his own he'd said he wouldn't be seen dead using it, in fact he'd asked his dad more than once not to use it in front of him.

Jim can't bear it. He rings Shirley, hoping Luke picks up the phone but he doesn't, why would he? He's got his own and he's not answering that.

He won't return my calls.

Jim says, not bothering with niceties like hello, how are you.

Where are you living? When can I come?

Look, Jim, he doesn't want to talk to you at the moment, let him come round, in his own time, it will blow over, these things usually do, things will get back to normal soon enough.

Secretly, Shirley loves this, loves the fact that the tables have turned. And as if reading her mind Jim says exactly that.

I bet you're enjoying this.

I don't have to take continual insults from you, Jim.

She says, putting down the phone.

I didn't handle that too well, he thinks.

What he'd really wanted to say was, he felt lonely, cut out and was missing his son. When Luke was a baby he'd sit in his high chair and say, pointing at his food:

I don't like that!

Well, Jim doesn't like this.

Where had those days, those years gone? The carrying on shoulders, the reading of a bedtime story, the playing with a ball in a park? Gone, with the orbit round the sun.

Jim empties a can of soup in a two day old dirty pan. He doesn't have the heart to cook or wash up properly now. His drinking glasses are turning green with mould. He leaves them in the sun to dry after washing them in cold water. He's down to cans, packets and bacon. Worse than that, he found himself pouring the fat from the grilled bacon into a cup and drinking it. Didn't know why, it sure wasn't a tonic, it tasted foul. He'd like to hibernate, but he can't do that. He isn't going to raise the white flag of surrender. He'd made an effort when Luke was around and he'd make an effort now. It had only been a matter of weeks and it felt like a lifetime. Shit, he'd start sorting his trip out, but the magic of that had already begun to fade.

Jim decides to get out. He walks down the road, turns the corner and meets a neighbour, a man whose hair he cuts. Whichever way he turns he can't get away from hair, heads and his scissors. They're everywhere, they're all around him.

The man's outside his house with his wife, building a boat, bits of it all over the place, it's tipped out like one massive jigsaw in the front garden, they work on The Ark every year when the weather's good and the nights are long.

He hears a lot of chatter about them, they're a couple that people like to gossip about, when there's nothing else to say, they're good gap fillers, the boat builders. If ever a conversation is running dry put a boat builder on top.

There might be bits of the boat in the bedrooms, the bathroom, out the back. Jim didn't know and nor did others. They're planning to sail off into the horizon, discover different countries, themselves and finally God, do some sort of missionary work. They talk about it very matter-of-factly, Jim doesn't know what sect they belong to or even if it's a sect at all. Might just be regular Christians trying to do a good thing.

Sorted out that jigsaw yet? Jim asks, looking at the crouching couple, they're always together.

Him and her in blue overalls, looking more like sailors every day.

Just a few pieces missing as you can see.

There are nuts and bolts, rope and rigging everywhere. The couple start to laugh. Jim looks at them, reckons they'd be good in a storm, good at capsizing, good going down. Good in the situation Jim's found himself in now. They had each other, nothing beat that.

Doesn't it come with instructions?

If it did, we lost them years ago, didn't we love?

The wife says, laughing.

He'd like to shake their hands, he really would, people were mistaken about this couple. Building a boat in your own front garden, not everyone gets around to doing that in a lifetime.

Jim had always found them more inspiring than odd.

Make sure that you come in for your farewell cut. Sorry, I don't do women but I could make an exception if you were going for a short back and sides.

Sure, why not.

She smiles and they get back to picking up nuts and threading bolts, they're too busy for any more natter, they've got a boat to be built and a God waiting for them to serve.

Back at home, Jim's thinking about them when the phone goes. It doesn't go that often in the house, he looks at it, hopes it's Luke, thinks that maybe Shirley has had a word after all, had a change of heart. Hopes it isn't someone selling insurance, banking or windows. It isn't, it's a woman. A voice he doesn't recognise even though she knows his name and uses it as if they've already met.

Hello Mr January, I'm the EWO officer, just…

The EWO?

Jim repeats, thinking shit, I should have paid that parking ticket after all, he's in dispute with the council and he knows he's in the wrong.

Just following up on Luke, so far he's not missed a day. I just wanted to congratulate you. The eight point plan must be working.

She doesn't really care if it has or hasn't, she shouldn't think like that but without truants she'd be out of a job. No, what she's phoned for is Jim. Since their meeting she can't stop thinking about him. Fantasising about the two of them, in a car together, he's ever so slowly undoing her buttons. Jim doesn't know this.

Oh, it's not really down to me. More my ex, actually.

Jim has to be honest, he hadn't seen his son, since she'd collected him, he doesn't even know their address. He'd waited outside the school gates one day, but felt uneasy about the looks he'd been given and walked quickly away. Hadn't been brave enough to give it another go. He knew how quickly rumours spread.

I don't believe that, not for a moment.

The EWO says. She loves the strong silent type, someone not full of himself. Not like Casanova back home, festering away on the sofa. She'd love a man who would see her as, dynamic, intelligent and beautiful.

Well, would it be possible to talk a few things over? To fill in a few of the missing gaps so to speak.

Gaps? Sure, where, when? What gaps?

Jim says, happy for the company, happy to be in conversation, happy to be doing something before his shutters went back down.

Formal or informal?

The officer asks.

Shit, I'm useless at formal. Sorry about swearing, see, I proved my point, I'm not very good at it.

Jim says, correcting himself.

Well alright, how about the school car park in, say, an hour.

She can't believe how easy he's been, if only teenage girls could realise, if only her teen self had realised how soft, how putty-like males really are.

An hour? Well alright, it's that important?

Oh, it's important alright.

She says, trying to convey her intention. It's lost on Jim, he's thinking about Luke, glad he's got his schooling back on track, glad to be involved in some small way, to be of some use, glad the officer called him instead of Shirley.

Jim uses his motorbike to ride to the school. The nights

are getting longer and warmer, it's a lovely evening and bits of insects are battering his visor. The EWO sees him approaching. Jim comes to a stop by the only car in the car park.

You teachers work some long hours don't you?

Jim says through his open visor, surprised that she's still working at six thirty. Shirley never had. You've gone and done it again the officer thinks, mistaken me for a teacher, you gorgeous man.

The trouble is we won't be able to get in. The caretaker must have locked up. It looks like I've wasted your time. That is unless you want to discuss it over a drink?

She'd only ever gone straight in for the kill like this twice before.

Jim looks at the woman. He hadn't spent a night in the company of a woman since his wife had left, he's sure he can smell her through the car window. Now here he was being asked out in a school car park, on his bike with his engine throbbing.

So can I take your silence as a yes, then?

Jim hadn't said a word, he's surprised by what's going on.

Yes sure, why not? I'm sorry, I'd love to, that'd be nice.

On your bike or in my car?

Well it's a nice night for a ride, I've got a spare helmet in the pannier, that's if you've been a pillion before?

Oh, I've been a pillion, in fact I was told I was good at it.

Before he knows it, she's on the back, helmet done up and they're riding along the lanes, the sun dipping behind the hedges.

He's got Luke's teacher on the back and he doesn't even know her name. It's only when he goes over a bump and she doesn't take her hand away from where it landed does Jim have a truer understanding of what is going on. He's nervous and it's too dangerous to move it. So he leaves it where it's settled. Shit, the last time he took Shirley out on the Rocket she'd demanded to go back home within minutes, Jim had only just missed a truck while overtaking. Shirley had thought that Jim wasn't up to riding, lacked the concentration and now here he was with a woman's hand bouncing around near his knob, fully alert and being careful with the throttle.

Over drinks in a country pub, Jim tells her the story of motorways and how, when they were first being built, people would watch sitting on deck chairs. On and on Jim goes, talking at speed, telling stories, spewing out any old pieces of junk he himself had been told. He just doesn't want silence. Silence would be the end of the night. So on and on he goes, like a late night disc jockey with nothing to say and a lot of hours in which to say it. He can't believe how nervous he is, he's sweating but he's enjoying himself and his leg is shaking. Judging from the look on her face he thinks she must be feeling the same.

He tells her about a man who writes a note to himself, every night before he goes to bed and on the note is written: DON'T SNORE.

The officer laughs about what she's just heard because that's what her Casanova would be doing right now, she checks her watch, she could set her clock to his first snore of the evening and the cat coming to lay on his lap.

She hadn't had children, not with that man and not with her first. She'd liked her figure too much, didn't want stretch marks, didn't want her prizes to swell then droop and drop and anyway now it was too late.

Jim's biggest problem, and he's thinking about it while he's talking, is how long has she had her hand on his thigh? He hadn't had a hand resting there in years. He can't believe a Monday night is panning out this way. Any more Monday nights like this and he'd believe in bloody miracles. Because there's no other way to describe it, what was going on here was a bloody miracle. Only a couple of hours before he'd been desperately drinking bacon fat.

After stories, laughter and a fun ride back, Jim's sitting

in her car, with the radio on. Jim notices the ads, he doesn't like ads on the radio and he tells her.

She turns to Jim, she's made her mind up, looks down at her breasts and says.

Forget about the ads, Mr January, you can look but you're not allowed to touch. One other thing, I want you to start calling me Fancy Pants.

Jesus, Jim thinks, how women have changed.

Now, remember, no hands.

Jim repeats the instructions, not really knowing what he is allowed to do.

Use your teeth and tongue and no cheating. Oi, hands away.

The evening takes on another twist.

What was it about teachers and him? Jim thinks. What was it about them and telling him what to do? What was it about him and them that he was now undoing buttons with his teeth?

There was nothing left in Wales for Karen, apart from being Welsh and that wasn't good enough for her. She'd left the valleys years ago to do what she wanted, she'd even ditched the accent. She had sisters back in the valleys living five doors down from where they were born. One to the left, one to the right of her ageing, dying, smoke infected parents.

Jim didn't even feel ridiculous as he was bobbing, because technically that's what he was doing, no hands. When he got home, he caught himself smiling in the mirror, it was the first time he hadn't thought of Luke in weeks. And then he thinks he'd better get those teeth cleaned, in case she gave him another chance. Because he bloody well hopes she will.

Chapter 20

Luke wasn't getting it so good, drowning not bobbing. What he doesn't realise is that moping around like a Neanderthal isn't helping. He can scratch his head all he likes, beat his chest, but its not helping his situation.

Shirley's not going to put up with any more of his teenage tantrums, his sulks, his silences, quite basically his titting around. He'd been spoilt, she saw the signs, knew the signals. She knew exactly how the problematic turned into full-blown idiots. Truth be told, she didn't particularly like teenage boys, they reminded her too much of her twin brother. All hopes, attention and time were pinned on him when they were young. He'd been like a prized, prancing, rosette-winning pony. He was the apple of her parent's eyes and they'd do anything to make sure he'd become a doctor. He'd done precisely that, more, he'd become a consultant. Her childhood was spent in a house that had been run for her twin's needs. Silence, conversation, laughter and games, according to his whims. Her own education was totally expendable if his needs came first. And what sort of uncle had he ever been to Luke? The last time he'd seen his nephew, he'd said:

When you stop growing, come and see me and I'll do something about your ears.

He privately educated his own. He didn't mind his twin working as a teacher but always wondered why she persisted with the public sector, why she'd not switched. Each and every Christmas, Shirley received the sickening round robin letter about all of his family's successes. She resented her twin and all that he'd become, resented the fact that her own childhood hadn't been valued, not worth as much as his. She remembers him trying to follow her, screaming because he couldn't keep up, her getting slapped because he'd fallen and cut his knee, she'd been made to watch as it was stitched. She remembers the hurts and the injustice of it all. She never forgave her parents nor her brother.

What Luke's got to understand is that he'd be sorry if he missed school again, sorry if he disobeyed her, sorry if he didn't stand up straight, sorry if he ever bad mouthed her again, sorry if he didn't show her respect. Sorry if he didn't get an education and sorry if he didn't make the mark. She'd make him sorry alright. When it came to dishing out sorrow, Shirley was the master.

Hadn't she been trying? Hadn't she been soft on the first night? Patient? Bought him pizza and tried to engage with his pathetic, moody silence? She hadn't said a negative word, she'd given him time. And what had she got in return? Absolutely nothing. Well, she wasn't going to be anyone's doormat, especially not her own son's, no, she'd given him more than enough time. Things were about to change.

Shirley likes extra strong mints, they keep her breath fresh and hot and clean. She buys them from the same shop every week, has done for years. The owner knows she's a teacher and likes to impress her with his arithmetic. He's good at it, he'll hold up one item, then another, milk, chocolate, gum, a paper, a can, adds them as quick as his till ever can. Gives a penny and pound answer. Then rings them up on the till, so she knows he's not cheating. She's genuinely impressed. It's a little game they play about once a month.

As Shirley opens the door today, she's neither in nor out, she sees the mathematician slap his wife hard on the side of her face. She's a small woman, with a red dot, gold earrings and a bright saree. He's hit her hard enough to leave a mark for the rest of the day. For Shirley it's a hallelujah moment, a flash to all her fears about Luke, it's a light bulb moment, she really hates that term. All that wasted potential behind the counter, among the porn and fags. His arithmetic is nothing but a party trick. Shirley realises what she's got to do, what she must do with her own son. A couple of hours a day is not enough. She's got to remove him from school and home educate him before he's lost to the hinterland of no hope, where 'potential' sat on litter strewn corners, like seagull chicks waiting on rooftops for mother to come back with fish. No child of hers was going to miss a proper education, not if she could help it, it was never too late for education. All it took was nurture, her nurture.

What on earth do you think you're doing, Mr Shyter?

She's never been able to pronounce his name. He's surprised and shocked to see her at the door. Secretly he's always wished his wife was more like her, he has his favourite customers and she's certainly one of them. He especially likes the way her bum moves as she leaves the shop.

I won't be buying my mints here again.

Shirley says, on her way out.

The first thing she did when she got home was confiscate Luke's phone, he stared in disbelief as it was taken from his hand. He'd wanted to hit her, she'd noticed his clenched fist but he was powerless to use it. The second thing to be withdrawn was his Xbox. The third thing was to get the attic sorted. She'd already made an appointment for builders to come round the following day.

If Jim wasn't man enough to discipline him, she certainly was. Luke may not be bothered about his own education but she'd sort him out if it was the last thing she ever did. And another thing, she's fed up with his hair, its long, lank, straight darkness. The way it hangs over his hunched shoulders, the way the ends dip into his cereal dish and the way he keeps on flicking it. Yes, that could go as well.

And why Jim hadn't attacked it yet, she'd never know.

Chapter 21

I'm made of china, Jim thinks, as he runs along the seafront, the wind blowing between his legs, seagulls watching him from a bin. He's blowing a bit himself and he's sure he can hear his hamstrings rattling, like an old lady carrying a tray full of china cups. He's sure if he fell over that he wouldn't bruise, he'd shatter, but it's a small price to pay.

Jim's getting in shape, he has to. He's been doing squats, stretches and shadow boxing. He's been busy, busy doing things that would have been unimaginable a couple of months ago. As he runs, a little smile appears on his face. For a moment he thinks everything is beautiful, everything is sparkling. Up the hill he runs, past the antique shops, the new café (someone else having a go, good on them) to the barbers. He fiddles with the lock wishing he could pick it, because he sure hates the key. It's something else he's made do with when he should have taken action. Action, my God, Karen likes her action, he thinks, slumping down onto a chair, legs sticking straight out like white lollypop sticks, sweat beads hitting the floor. Just thinking about Karen makes him tired. What was last night all about, anyway? He shakes his head. He'd been made, well not exactly forced, to crawl around naked with her, his good lady, in jockey silks on his back. I'm a grown man, he thought, as he went round and round with his jockey on top. He's got carpet burns on his knees to prove it. He'd wanted to shout, Stop, stop I can't take it anymore but he hadn't.

Truth be, he'd quite liked her slapping his arse and the feel of the silk on his skin.

There's a pounding on the door, it's not yet ten and the sign's still showing closed. Jim pops out from his jockey thoughts, looks up to see a young man, with no hair. He'd have to use a sander or a chisel to do any work there.

I'm closed.

Jim shouts, points to the clock, thinking, what does he need from me that shoe polish couldn't do?

I know, I'm good with signs.

Good.

The young man's on a mission. Likes to get things done, won't settle until they are, he's obsessive in that way. His mum's the same, worse.

Jim gets up to have a wash. He feels naked sitting in his red shorts, perspiring like a whore in an Amsterdam window. He'd been pretty much panting since he met Karen, she'd turned him a little crazy. The young man pounds again, louder.

Alright, alright, I'm shut, I've already told you.

Jim says, getting annoyed.

It's about Danny. He was a friend of mine.

Danny?

Jim looks at the young man, what does he know about Danny? Jim walks to the door, turns the lock.

Danny Sloane.

Jim hadn't thought about Danny, not since Shirley had taken his son and Karen had got on his back. He suddenly feels guilty again. The thing is, Jim's been busy, his knees and back are paying a terrible price, he's already booked for a chiropractic crack. He still doesn't know Shirley's new address or where Luke is. It's something else he's got to sort out, he thinks, looking at the young man. I've got to get my priorities right. But there's no denying playing horses was more fun.

What about Danny?

Jim says, standing there in his tight shorts, his running vest, all he needs is a number and he'd look ready for a marathon. He feels a little undressed.

He was a good friend of mine. I live in New Zealand, Danny and I Skyped. He showed me round this place. Funny, the shop looked bigger on Skype.

Jim extends his hand.

So, you are?

Carl. We were in the army together. I ended up going to New Zealand to lick my wounds and he ended up in a box. What have you done to your knees, mate?

Carl's already picked up a rising inflection.

Carpet burns. So you're the one who went off to find space?

Danny talked a lot about you.

He's sure Danny had said he was an amputee.

Carl catches Jim's eye movement, looking down below.

Hardly tell, ha?

Jim has to admit it's hard to spot. He only knows one other cripple, he comes in on his burgundy mobility

149

cart, flying a pirate's flag. He's a tanner, loves the sun, loves it like a Christian loves a bible. He works his tan at the St Leonard's end and has a competitor a mile up the prom, working Hastings. They tan all summer then a judge decides the winner. They'd asked Jim one year, he'd found it hard to pick a winner.

Carl's missing leg unsettles Jim, it cripples his flow. He doesn't want to say cripple, broken, bent, any words like that. He's the same when he talks to men of colour, he doesn't like mentioning the colour black, doesn't like it when he says things like: black temper, black thoughts, black coffee, black sheep of the family. Thinks he might sound racist. He's going to have to be careful here, avoid words like missing, broken, hop, knackered, fucked up.

If Jim was being frank, he reckoned he'd developed his fear of the English language from years of diplomacy, hiding his true feelings from his customers and not wanting to slip up.

Excuse me, Carl, I'm just going to get changed.

Jim takes his carpet burns behind the curtain. As he's changing, Carl carries on.

I got into shearing in Z. Similar to your game, I guess, just bigger clippers.

Yeah, Danny was keen to give it a go, he only practiced on humans so he could get to sheep.

We're all bloody sheep mate, every last one of us.
Carl says from the other side of the curtain.

Jim decides not to comment. Danny had said something very similar.

That's better.

Jim says, in his barbers coat, feeling freer to talk, more professional, definitely more able to concentrate now his own knees were covered up.

So what can I get you, a cup of tea, coffee, coke? You sure don't need a cut.

No, I'm fine. I'm not really here for tea.

And he brings out a folded piece of paper and taps it.

I'm here because of this.

His thirst for revenge comes from his mum's side of the family. He was her only child, his dad hadn't stuck around. Carl's mum had collected a black bin bag's worth of dirty nappies and shoved as many of them through the absent father's letter box as she could before they got bunged up. He'd recently taken up with a new lady and she'd wanted to let her know that she could forget about any rosy future and especially, and this was the important bit, forget about any gurgling kids.

Someone's got to pay.

Jim reckons the young man is holding a bill.

Did Danny owe you money?

Jim looks at the young man, another lost soul standing in front of my mirrors, he thinks.

Danny thought you were alright. He said so in his letters. That's why I'm here really, just to say thanks, thanks for trying to help my friend. For giving him an opportunity, I know he appreciated it.

Jim looks at the young man, he's still confused.

Well, I obviously didn't do enough.

He should have come to Z with me when he had the chance. Then he wouldn't have had to go and kill himself would he?

Jim hadn't been told if it was suicide or not. No-one had been sure, not even Charlie Sloane. He'd left a message for Jim on his answer phone a week ago, another one that Jim hadn't responded to. All Charlie had said was:

Still reading, still finding things out.

He hadn't rung back because he was scared to. If Jim was being truthful, he was enjoying his new state of mind, not having dark thoughts, happy playing a pony late into the night. He hadn't returned the call because he wanted to protect that. It was selfish, it was the truth, Jim couldn't take anymore woes.

Carl offers his hand, it was nice to meet you.

How about a cup of tea before you go?

Jim makes a move towards the kettle.

I've never really been much of a talker or tea drinker.

He's sure of himself, for a young man. He offers his hand again and as quickly as he appeared, the soldier was gone. Gone before the clock had struck ten. Jim watches him walk down the street with hardly a limp at all.

He comes back into the shop to hear a text arriving.

Just two words,

Be Ready.

God only knows what they'd be getting up to tonight.

Chapter 22

Carl had done his research. It wasn't hard. Twitter and Facebook had left a slug's slimy trail to Danny's brother, Joseph, the beater, the bully, the bastard. A trail to where he drank, what he drank, what time he drank it, what he'd just drunk, drivel. It was all there in his frantic tweeting texting, finger world. Carl spent a night online looking at Joseph, blogging his innards out.

It was more than enough. Carl had switched in to operational mode, he liked getting focused, sorting options out. That's what he'd liked most about the army, the structure, the rules, knowing what was happening tomorrow and the day after that. If he hadn't lost a leg he'd still be signed up. What was life without a purpose? Since the amputation, he hadn't found the answer.

Danny's last letter had changed that.

Out of respect he visits his dead friend's parents. Carl thought it would be the right and proper thing to do, the Sloanes deserved that. He knocks.

Mrs Sloane comes to the door, looking old, minus a son, like the mother she now is. She talks through the chained door. She didn't take chances with her lonely life.

Hello, I'm Carl, Danny's mate from the army.

She slides the lock and calls out for Charlie.

Charlie, there's someone here to see us.

She needs her husband to come down to be by her side. She hated dealing with strangers, the phone ringing was bad enough. She'd take it as incoming, expecting the enemy on the line.

Charlie. Come down.

She shouts in panic. Carl can hear her panic but manages to hold his smile, tries to look friendly.

Please come in, but if you don't mind, will you take your shoes off?

She'd always been clean but she's become obsessive since her son died. It's what she did with her time now apart from the sewing, cleaned from carpet to cornice. Trying to wash it all away, the dirt, the pain, for it all to be gone.

Danny takes one shoe off and then says:

I think it would be better if I left this one on.

He knew that if he took it off, he'd have to tell the story. How he lost it and all the other questions which come rumbling along. Carl wished his leg could tell its own story. Better still, a prosthetic with bullet points, commentary, charts, maps and a little film.

What a strange boy, Mrs Sloane thinks, desperate now for her absent husband to appear. She invites the strange boy into the living room, points to a chair.

Charlie comes down carrying a handful of diaries. He walks around with them, doesn't even know he's doing it. He's aged, hasn't taken his son's death well. He's short in concentration, short in temper, short in sentences. He spends hours in his Danny's room, more time now than when his son was alive, sitting, reading, stroking the diaries, mourning the death of his youngest. Sometimes he pulls some of his clothes out and smells them or just lies on his dead son's bed, like it's a coffin.

Hello Mr Sloane, I'm Carl.

Oh, hello Carl, it's good to meet you, Danny wrote a lot about you.

Charlie says, handing him a diary. Carl knew Danny was a diarist, he used to watch him in his cot, scribbling under torch light, wishing he could do the same but he wasn't the type. He'd worry that he'd have nothing to remember the war by, he shouldn't have. A couple of weeks later he was minus a leg, being helicoptered out. Woke up to hear hospital managers talking about the cost of the bed he was lying in. Other soldiers walking up and down in a trance, with blown faces and minds, necks in traction, missing arms.

What Carl needed, knew he needed, then as he does now, is space, space to think, space where he can heal his body, his mind.

The Sloanes are looking at him in silence, they don't know what to say.

It's an honour, a complete honour, Son.

Charlie says, finding words, biting into his biscuit, sending shards into the room, they kept them in a tin for occasions like this, not that they had many. Their eldest hardly ever appeared and when he did it was usually with forms to be filled, which they did in a semi-trance. The few friends they did have hadn't been back since the day of the funeral. It was too awkward for all concerned, so they were left alone with their suffering and sorrow.

After an appropriate period of silence, Carl said that he'd better get going what with there being a ferry to catch and all.

Goodbye, then.

Bye.

Carl says and salutes them. He has no idea why.

They stand at the door and watch Carl's departing back. Mrs Sloane turns to her husband.

How strange, why do you think he only takes one shoe off?

Charlie knows the answer, it's in the diaries.

Maybe he's got athlete's foot.

Oh, that's a good point, dear.

She trusts her husband, maybe they'd be alright, after all, she thinks. They turn and go into what was once a family house for four.

Chapter 23

Mr Sloane made a call to Joseph and invited him over. He lied, said that he and his mum would love to see him. Finished up with more false words.

I can't wait to see you, Son.

It sickened him. He's been reading about his oldest in the diaries, it wasn't pleasant reading. It described the beatings, the fear, the anxiety and pain he'd caused his younger brother. The diaries were slowly killing him, he'd save his wife from the worst of it. He'd started removing pages, leaving them under a loose floorboard.

Joseph, the beater, the bastard (he'd happily use those terms to describe himself) arrives carrying a bag over his shoulder, pamphlets in his hand and a cross swinging around his neck (reckons it makes him look more honest, helps close the deal). He's ready for business. Charlie enticed him with insurance talk, business talk, talk about money, talk he liked. He'd invited him to come around on the only day of the week that his mum went out shopping.

She was out at Iceland, they ate frozen now. She'd be out until the cab brought her back with her frozen packs and the cold chill she travelled with inside.

Man talk. Charlie called it, as they took seats at opposite ends of the table, Charlie sliding the biscuit tin towards his son. He didn't want their hands to touch.

So, how you been, Son?

A pause before saying Son. He feels he's betraying the word and all that it stands for. He would love to give up on him, he really would. Tell him he wasn't wanted or welcome in the house anymore. See him walk away for good.

But if he did, what would he have left? A broken partner, a husk of a life.

I'm fine, Dad and you?

Joseph doesn't need to ask. It's more than apparent that his dad's awash. If he was a ship, he'd be hearing the mayday call, if he was a spitfire he'd be heading for the hay. He feels nothing. Why should he? What had his dad ever really done for him? The only piece of advice he's ever remembered from his dad is to squeeze toothpaste from the bottom.

Joseph's view of the world was simple. Some people were sharks and some weren't, Joseph was a shark and he was circling.

Charlie looks at his son and wonders where it all went wrong. Sitting in front of him at the end of the wooden table, flowers and biscuits in between, he loathes him. After a sickening silence, he speaks.

Why, Son? Why?

He can't do eye contact. Hasn't been able to, since Joseph entered the house. He's only looked at his face once, fleetingly.

Why, what?

Joseph thinks he's talking about the increased life insurance premiums. He'd talked about it on the phone, but he'd been unable to make himself clear. Hence him sitting here, a blue folder in his hands, with numbers, flows and dividends. He touches his cross, he does it before he talks about money, before deals. He's worn it for years. If it was DNA tested there'd be some of his brother on it.

I just think it would be good for you and Mum to take out some more cover. I couldn't bear to think of either of you in some shitty nursing home, a place where no-one cared.

He couldn't, the thought of them eating up the house in nursing home fees has cost him many hours of sleep. It isn't the real reason and Charlie knows it, the games up. He wouldn't have known that three months ago. He does now. He's learnt more in the last months about his boys, than he'd done in Danny's lifetime.

Joseph hadn't shed one tear about his brother's suicide, not one. Couldn't even force one out for the final going down the hole show. Charlie had noticed, thought he'd been strong, brave, brazened it out for them, on that day he'd been proud of him.

Joseph may not have cried at the lowering of the box but he had seen a ghost from his past. He'd hoped she was already dead of some cancer, which had slowly eaten her insides away.

When he'd seen her at the funeral with that smile, the familiar smile from his youth, he was shocked, taken back to the terror of his schooldays.

On his very first day at school, she'd made him sit on his own. He'd already been singled out. Sat at the front with his nose touching a wall. Newly painted he'd sat there frightened, smelling the paint.

Who invited that teacher, Dad? Why was she at the funeral?

Joseph asks, surprising his dad. Charlie doesn't like hearing the word Dad come from his son's mouth now.

What teacher? What are you talking about?

The teacher.

Joseph shouts.

I don't know a teacher.

He doesn't. He and Jim January might drink together but they sure hadn't met each other's wives.

The Sloanes let teachers teach, they'd not stepped a foot in a school more than three times in both of their sons' educations. They hadn't wanted to interfere, they weren't that type. They knew other parents that did. Let teachers teach and parents parent, was more their motto.

Joseph had been ritually humiliated by that teacher, made to stand up front, to stand outside, picked on and bullied. He'd had pictures ripped from books and his thoughts shot down before they were even fully out. What had Joseph done?

Nothing, he was a child. The woman had tormented him, cut his learning shoots, choked him off and like a cut flower he'd slowly wilted, died in his seat staring at his desk. What had he been trying to do ever since? Prove himself, prove himself to his parents, prove himself to the world.

Perhaps she'd made him the man he now was. He'd

thought she was dead, buried and forgotten. She wasn't. She'd come back. She was standing there in black, something familiar in her smile, her lopsided grin.

Not the eyes, not the face. No, what he recognised, what he'd never forgotten, was the sound of her voice and that smile. Everything else had aged, gone to seed, the eyes, the hair, the skin, but not the voice or smile. It still had the same haunting pitch, sending him back to the darkness, back to his childhood, back to the day it had started.

Charlie looks at his son, at his face, at his suit, looks at the son he's created. He'd thought about the next question, thought about it long and hard. First of all he'd thought, how could he ask it? Then how could he not, so he asks once more.

Why?

Why what?

Why?

It's the exact question Joseph wants to ask the teacher. He's got a lot of whys he wants to ask.

Joseph's found where she lives, it wasn't hard. He'd followed her back from his old school, him in his car, her in hers. He couldn't believe she still taught there, hadn't anyone complained? Had he been the only one?

He'd pulled up at a red light by the side of her and stared. She hadn't turned, just kept her eyes out front, waiting for the lights to change.

You do that lady, wait for your lights to change.

Joseph had shouted. He'd change her lights so they stayed on red forever.

Chapter 24

Miss Petticoat, Shirley is on the phone, talking to the Head of her school. Asking for compassionate leave, giving her reasons as to why she'll need perhaps another month, more than the week she's already taken. She's lying, saying her son's got an illness, meningitis, it's down on his records, had it as a youngster, always needs to be watched. She doesn't want to take any chances, doesn't want any other pupils to run the risk of catching it. The Head agrees entirely, no-one wants that. Shirley will take the time with or without the young Head's consent, but he doesn't know that. She doesn't care what he's got to say but she's agreeing, saying 'exactly' in all the right places. She's learnt to listen carefully, not get caught out. He's talking about cover and if there is anything else that can be done to help. This is his first Headship. He'd worked hard to get it, he wasn't a natural choice, but somehow he'd got the job. He'd loved putting the wooden Head Teacher sign on the door announcing to the world his arrival, showing the doubters. He's full of new ideas and directions he wants the school to take. Mostly, he likes the sound of his own voice. What he doesn't want to do is lose a good member of staff, because if he knows one thing, he knows when he's got one. He's seen her with the kids, the way she gets them to interact, the way she gets them interested, the fun they seem to be having. Learning should be fun, didn't she agree? She did. It was one of his little mantras. If he could have he'd have hung a little sign around his neck, or had it printed all over one of his bright coloured, wacky ties.

Luke's looking down at his mother using the phone. He's all concentration, all ears now. He's been excluded from his school. He doesn't know the real reason but thinks it has something to do with never having his shirt tucked in and dying his hair black. He's full of focus now, his eyes hurt from moving them this way and that. Luke can't talk anymore, not that he talked much before, but now he really can't. Things have changed. This isn't because he's chosen to remain silent, not like before, with his sullen sulks. He's not stropping now.

The trouble with Luke is, he's got a tea cloth balled up in his mouth and it tastes foul. His mum put it there and not because he didn't help with the dishes. Not because he swore. No, it's there as a learning aid, a prompt. It's held in place with gaffa tape so it doesn't fall out, doesn't go anywhere. It's hurting his ears and getting caught in his hair. Most of all it makes breathing difficult. His mum has got him enrolled on a new syllabus, her syllabus. If Luke had to describe it he'd say it was fucking mad.

The tea towel is in his mouth so he can't interrupt,

can't shout, can't cause a commotion when she's using the phone or if she goes out. If that isn't bad enough (which it is) he's cuffed to the iron bed head as well, his wrist's already swollen, puffed up and cut, he's become a character in one of his Xbox games. He's pounded on the door and hit the wall. He's all but nearly given up. He's never had much tenacity, sure not had stamina, he'd never seen the point, wishes he had it now.

Luke would love to talk about his predicament, talk to anyone. He could be really quite expansive now. What he wants to do most is open his mouth and holler, blub and be what he really is; a scared boy locked away in an attic, afraid of his mum's attention, her temper and her strange teaching methods.

He regrets that he hasn't got a real friend, someone who'd care if he was missing from school, maybe go round to his dad's to look for him.

The last time he saw or spoke to his dad he was throwing him a sign and telling him to F off out of the departing car's window. He'd not once returned one of his many calls. He's regretting that now, chained to the bed with a stinking tea towel in his mouth (he's sure it's had olives on it).

He tried to break free, rattled his hand, bit at it, but that hurt his teeth and then tried to wriggle out like a magician. Nothing worked and eventually, like most things he'd tried, he gave up.

His relationship with Molly, his girlfriend, had broken down. She wouldn't be missing him. His mistake, he'd put his hands up to that (if he could, he can't). It happened the first time he left the security of tongues and teeth colliding. Came out of his trench and went over the top for one of her tits. It was a padded affair and it embarrassed her as he came away holding a rolled up pink sock. She didn't have big enough breasts to fill the bra she'd coveted. The first thing she was going to do with a wage packet was to get her breasts enlarged. She'd already told her mum, who'd nodded in total agreement. She didn't care if they leaked or not, she wanted one thing, for them to be bigger.

He doubts if anyone's missing him out there in the Facebook world, for all he knows he might have been clicked off, un-clicked, no longer in the digital world. No-one would be worrying about his lack of updates. If he got a chance to get near a machine, near a phone, he'd tell them, he'd surprise a few now.

In the attic chained to a bed with tea towel stuffed in my mouth, OMG. Mum gone well mad. LOL. SMH.

He'd get some traffic with that type of posting. What if everyone just thought it was a joke? Or that he was some sort of emo.

The loft conversion consisted of some electrical wiring and a lot of hardboard banged down to make a floor, all done in three days by a man who was quick with a saw and only dealt in cash. No guarantee came with the job, but he did throw in loft ladders at cost price, so you could get in and out of the place. The landlord, if he'd been asked (he hadn't) wouldn't have minded her tampering with his roof. He never came round. He liked his empire, his operation, his portfolio, to run itself. He specialised in low maintenance. He'd been the same with his wives, he'd had three already and he's not even hit fifty. Romance and conversation were saved for courtship.

Shirley had asked Luke if he wanted it as his own room. He'd agreed without hesitation, it was a no-brainer (his words). Sure, he'd said, in that 'I'm not bothered can't be arsed' tone that he'd perfected.

He'd wanted to be as far away from his mum as he could. He'd already picked her as a psycho, and now the cracks had really started to appear. She'd started shouting at him in some strange language, he didn't understand a word. He does now, it was bloody Latin.

The first thing Shirley did when she'd manoeuvred him into the situation was to cut his lank black hair so that he could see and hear her properly and when he eventually returned to school he wouldn't be referred to the refusal unit. She did it in his sleep after she'd applied the cuffs. She'd tried them out on her dancer. Luke had been surprised (much like the dancer) when he'd woken up in them. Really regrets being a good sleeper now, he'd always been told he was a heavy one. If he ever gets out, he's promised himself never to sleep well again.

In the windowless loft he could scream and shout and it wouldn't make any difference to the outside world. Shirley's checked and so has Luke. On waking with his wrist attached, Luke had gone berserk, shouted, banged and then like a tantruming toddler had run out of puff. She'd already checked on noise levels by blasting out a radio. Nothing could be heard from the street.

Miss Petticoat had been wise in choosing the sturdy brick building. She'd not once heard, never mind seen, her only neighbour. She'd knocked, tried to make contact, invite whoever to tea or coffee. Her conclusion was that they must collect their post early, live abroad or just detest company.

Shirley had teaching to get on with. Some children just needed a controlling hand, even if it took chaining and force-feeding, she'd get him learning, get him enlivened. Focus was what was needed now. Old-fashioned concentration and rote learning. This was her school now, a school for one and she'd use all of her tools to bring him on. She'd be his mentor even if it meant using a touch of passive force, she'd get him interested, listening and learning. She hasn't gone to all this trouble to simply torture her son.

As far as she's concerned he's been floating around in the land of mediocrity for years, coasting in the mire. It was high time for him to WAKE UP, for her to squeeze out his juice, his potential.

She'd thought long and hard before applying the cuffs. Seven nights she'd stood at the end of the bed, contemplating, before she'd done it.

She gets Luke to learn Latin phrases first thing in the morning, while he's fresh, three, maybe four, depends on his effort levels. She hopes it might help with his English, give him a deeper understanding of the roots of language. He isn't bothered. She'd love him to go to Oxford but up until this point he'd shown absolutely no aptitude, any university would do, really.

Luke doesn't see the point, as he's already said to his mum. He has enough trouble remembering the words he wants to use in English, never mind bloody Latin. Shirley's tried to explain, but gets exasperated.

This isn't easy for me.

Shirley has said more than once, tiring during a morning session, getting tetchy.

What, and this is?

He'd rattle his chain. She'd calmly state that she really did think he needed a helping hand and that it was all for the best, he'd see.

Ten weeks maximum. You'll see what a difference that makes.

That's exactly why she'd taken the drastic decision to micromanage her son. He was an embarrassment at school, wasting teachers' time. It went against everything Shirley stood for, hence the drastic measures, cuffs, tea towel and the ancient language lessons.

History follows Latin, then Geography, maybe some Maths. Shirley's not great at Maths. She's always had trouble trying to convey its complexities, she's not that good at teaching beyond primary level.

She's endeavouring to make him more able to cope with the outside world. More rounded. She'll use all she has in her professional teacher's tool box to see the job through.

Shirley's had similar conversations with other parents. Luke's never been the most interested or engaged. As far as she was concerned he had some catching up to do and if that took a little rocket up his arse and cuffs on his wrists, so be it.

If he does well, he earns stars on a chart. Shirley made it, uses similar ones at school. They incentivise, well they do with nine-year-olds. Stars represent treats; treats mean TV time for whatever channel he wants. His Xbox has been removed. She's cancelled the broadband and had the landline disconnected. The only way to the outside world is through her palm, through her phone. She never lets it out of sight, it locks within a second. She's on top of the situation, stupidity and forgetfulness wouldn't bring her down. Because her downfall would be his, whether he knew it or not. She'd get his brain ready.

She's stopped seeing her dancer, she'd had her last midnight tango, it was nice, it was tender and his ticker hadn't shut down when she'd applied the cuffs, after his surprise came arousal.

She closes and bolts the loft at ten thirty sharp, that's when he's told to sleep. She's had to go up there more than once to ask him to stop banging and screaming. She takes away privileges if he does, removes stars. One thing about these bizarre goings on is that his spots are drying up, all of them, from his bottom to his head. If any friend was to meet him now they'd have to say:

Fuck me, you've changed.

And they wouldn't be wrong. He's changed alright.

Chapter 25

Jim's on the phone to Karen finalising the bike trip. He's just noticed he's got an erection, they tend to appear when he's talking to his little Welsh dragon. There's no denying it, she turns him on.

He's excited, not because of her voice or what she's been doing to him at night, or in the afternoon, when he's had to turn the sign and pull the blinds. No, he's excited because his dream is getting closer. All those years it's been waiting for him and now the leaving time is approaching. He's going to hit the starter switch, swing his leg over the saddle and finally be off. He's got a lot of excitement in his veins. He's happy, happier than in years, happy to have been given another chance, happy to have found happiness again. He'd forgotten a feeling like this existed. It's taken years off his face.

He's sorted travel bags and panniers. What's in and what's not. He's hacksawed toothbrushes so they fit and made a first-aid kit, added a needle and thread. He's done a dummy run, packed and unpacked, made sure it all fits, it does. There's a website Jim used to see what was needed. There's a website for everything. He might even use one to find his long lost son because he sure isn't answering his calls.

He's sorted out passports and visas (Russia and Ukraine). They're going to ride to China along the old silk route, along the Great Wall. He'd read about it in a *National Geographic*, followed that with a series on DVD. He's going to give the dream he held out to Danny a shot, he still doesn't know if he should have offered it. He still hadn't heard whether it was suicide or not. Charlie Sloane had been quiet for months and Jim knows he should have rung but he hasn't. He really didn't want anything chasing away his good fortune, his good luck.

Karen hadn't needed much tempting, she'd jumped at it as soon as the sentence was out. She fancies gripping onto Jim and going as far as they get. Money's not a problem, she's got some saved up and what's it for, anyway? What else was she doing with her life? Apart from leaving an indentation in a sofa. She's bought a sort of phrase book, no words just hundreds of pictures to point at when in need, she's excited.

Her only luxury will be a nice glossy red lipstick. Jim reckons he can accommodate that, says she can have two. Karen said she wouldn't go without it, he said he wouldn't go without her.

She still hadn't told Jim that she wasn't a teacher. Not

that he'd asked, not that he'd care, but she hadn't. The only thing Jim might say over a pint, about his new lady, might whisper to a very, very close friend (if he had one) was that, how could he put it… ? Well, that she's a little bit you know, experimental and he didn't mean it in a bad way.

He'd become fitter and leaner than he'd been in years, goes around throwing punches at imagined enemies. Jim's been doing this trick with his testicles that prolong his coming. Karen showed him, she does this thing with her hand. He's a good student, he practices in the shower, practices by the kettle when no-one's around, doesn't have a clue as to how it works but work it bloody does.

If you asked Jim, even if you didn't, he reckoned he'd turned the bloody clock back years. He'd bought himself some 70's disco albums to boogie to at night. He'd even heard himself muttering, Oh, yeah, on his last mounting. Karen had turned and smiled, spurring the rodeo rider on. God he loved life at the moment. And what's wrong with that? What the hell was wrong with that? He'd asked himself plenty of times; the thing was, it still took some getting used to.

Karen's only problem might be the Casanova resting on his sofa back at the casa leaving his own sofa imprint and nail clippings. He loves to do them in front of the TV on a Sunday night, getting ready for the coming week.

She hadn't told him yet, she thought she'd leave it to the

last moment. She couldn't bear it if he cried or tried to hold her back, she might just punch him if he did that. She didn't want that as his final parting gift, him looking up from the floor. To soften the blow she'd bought him a year's subscription to Sky (she'd never previously allowed it in the home). As a going away present, as a goodbye kiss, a whole year's subscription to arse sitting.

She'd had it connected up in the spare room, he wouldn't see it. He hadn't been that far down the hall in years. She'd done it at her own expense. All he'd have to do is run a cable down to the junction box. She joined him up to his favourite football channel. He could spend hours watching all the gossip, all he does is read about it now. She reckoned it would take at least a month before he really noticed that she'd gone. It will give her the summer, if she throws in some freezer meals as well. She'd been cooking double of everything recently, his favourites. He'd already asked why the shopping bill had gone up so dramatically. He checks the house finances on a Saturday night before his lucky numbers are called. It's the type of thing he likes to do. It's the type of thing she's bored of.

She'd figured he really wouldn't care as long as he had something going to his eyes and into his mouth of an evening. She's not heartless, a little of her still cares but it's just over. She's going to lead him to the spare room, show him his gift, leave instructions for his dinners and then be gone. She hopes he has tears in his eyes, not because of her departure but because of his joy of Sky.

Jim, you won't mind if I send a postcard from all the different places we go to, will you?

She hoped he wouldn't mind, wouldn't be offended but she can't see his face, they're on the phone.

Of course not.

They're still at the stage where whatever one says there's total agreement. Jim's done arguments and doesn't want to do them again. No, whatever she wants is fine by Jim.

We could also send a car sticker with it. He could stick them on your car.

Fridge more like.

Karen can't see him putting them on a bumper, it would bring the value down, if he ever got round to selling it. He's mentioned it more than once, how he fancied driving something different. She didn't see that happening.

You know people sell them on eBay.

Jim says, he'd once thought about buying a few interesting countries and sticking them on his own bike, give it a bit more character.

Some people are just born cheats.

Karen says, knowing that's exactly what she's become,

a cheat.

Her husband had given up on humans in his forties and that included her, it had taken her a few years to realise but he had. The only thing he really talked to now were his fish. He feeds them at night. He's got a neon tank full of tropical fish that are attached to the wall and lit by a light. Soon they will be his only company, she hopes he has a favourite, he sure looks at them enough to have picked one.

I still feel a bit strange about taking another man's wife away on a trip.

Don't. Lets not talk about that.

He hadn't told his punters yet but he's told the wage sucking utilities companies. Gas, electric, things like that. God it felt good telling them that he wouldn't be needing their services, that he was going away.

Someone else had been walking away, not coming to school again. He's got a week's worth of crosses where ticks should be.

Karen's worried that if she tells Jim they won't go.

She needn't have, Shirley told Jim that Luke had meningitis again.

Chapter 26

Carl, the ex-soldier, is in a café, drinking coke, it's a Panda cola, not even a real one. The owner buys them in bulk and switches the can to a glass and hopes the customers don't notice. They do, Carl's noticed, it's in the fizz, the colour, the taste. The owner makes his mark-up on the can, does the same with his bacon, buys it in massive plastic packets, has trouble browning it because of the high water and whatever else content. He's never yet managed to get it crispy and by fuck he's tried. He's not a natural cook, he'd spent years in a car dealership running the spares department. The café is his last throw of the dice. He'd spent a year without work, too old to be employed by anyone else, taken a gamble, used all his own savings and was employing himself. His own family wouldn't eat in the café, they knew what he was like. He had Haynes manuals and pictures of car parts on the wall. He misses the spares department, he really does.

Carl's eating the bacon under two injured slabs of white bread. He pulls a long piece out, he's having trouble chewing it, thinks he could be on it all day, it would make a starling choke.

He's spent longer in this run down coastal town than he'd meant to, drunk too many Pandas. His target had disappeared for a week, not disappeared exactly, he'd told the world where he was going, Spain for a week. Spain for the two S's was how he put it on his Facebook updates. Sun and Sex.

So Carl waited, with the gulls flying high and the pedal swans going round and around in a small man-made lake with tired children on board.

He'd never been to a place where so many people were jostling for a position to ask for a pound or where the population were so ugly. Carl doesn't give money as a rule, he's the one with the one leg after all. He's already done his bit for Queen and country and taken a bullet. Not that people would know that as he walks around in his Ben Sherman shirt, his Lee jeans, setting himself smartly apart.

The torn pages from Danny's diary had come pre-warning him of his friend's demise. A small covering letter had been written on blue airmail paper. He'd been outside with a thousand sheep, minutes before the thin paper had arrived wrapped around the pages of the torn diary.

After reading it, he'd immediately made a call, it wasn't

Danny who answered, it was Charlie, sniffling, spluttering, gasping. It was the middle of the night and his friend's father's pain had just begun.

There was only one thing Carl wanted after reading Danny's pages, it was REVENGE. Danny's last line on the paper, last line to flow while he still had life as far as Carl was concerned, was:

A hit and run would be nice.

Carl didn't know if he was asking him or God to do it. He didn't intend on waiting for God.

With the letter had come a fishing hook, which Carl had already used to catch smaller, less troublesome fish in the sea while he waited for the big one. Mackerel, no skill or expertise needed. Just good soap to clean the stink off your hands afterwards.

Chapter 27

Joseph's having trouble with the air machine on the garage forecourt, it's taken his money but not giving air, not giving him what he's purchased, the fucking thieves. He loathes air machines. He's removed all his valve caps in preparation, to save time, to get the most out of his fifty pence worth. So the air doesn't run out half way through. And now after all this prep, all this organisation, it's not working. He feels angry and, as if answering his call, a young man with tattoos honks his car horn at him and flicks his hand as he would do at a fly. It's a blessed moment for Joseph. He'd already noticed how close the man had pulled up, it's a welcome distraction.

What, me?

Joseph's seen the film and does his best impersonation, he's always thought he had a bit of the Robert De Niro lurking deep inside.

What? You honking at me?

He says, letting the air hose go, it flies back, banging to a stop at the machine.

It's this exact reason why the machine never works, the forecourt manager thinks, watching from his glass perch, checking his CCTV camera is on and then going back to stack a few more Mars bars. The forecourt manager doesn't drive himself, but thinks that it must be very sugary work, because of all the drinks and chocolate consumed by drivers. That or headache inducing, he sells twenty packs of paracetamol a day. He's never got over the Englishman's need for them. Sometimes he thinks customers confuse them with mints.

The honker is an estate agent.

I don't see anyone else, Bud.

Smiles and leans out his window as he says it, he uses Bud to everyone now, it used to be Fella and before that Dude, his sentences are splattered with the latest terms. He's completely unaware of the impending danger. He thinks showing his tattooed arms is enough, that and being big and powerfully overweight. He's always thought that just falling on somebody would be enough to end a fight. That's the type of self-defence he'd teach or go to. Somewhere he could just fall down and sleep.

Joseph walks back to the machine and it unexpectedly comes back to life, vibrating and hissing. It's got air. He isn't going to waste the air or his luck. He picks it up and starts to pull it like a fireman working a hose in a hurry. The young estate agent is throbbing away in his double exhausted car, listening to a little drum and bass. He's close enough for Joseph and the hose to reach, which isn't a good thing. He's got a small house he's trying to let and it's problematic, because simply put, it's a bit of a shit hole. He's running late and he has a slow puncture. He's had it for over a month, uses the air machine twice a week instead of getting it fixed.

What you need is a nose enema, mate.

What?

The estate agent asks, thinks it might be something like a plaster for his puncture.

I'll show you if you like.

And Joseph does, he pulls the man's head forward and releases the trigger at the same time, the metal end scratches his nasal passage and air shoots to his brain, it's a direct hit, a brain rattler. The estate agent forces himself back and splutters. It's an odd thing to happen at any point in one's day and it's all over quickly, he's never had air hit his brain with such force before. Nauseating and dark is how it mainly feels.

Fuck that hurts.

He shouts, slamming his car into reverse, getting five

metres away from the maniac with the hose. He doesn't know if he should put it in first and slam the tanned fucker. If it wasn't for the fact he wanted to get on, make some money and not spend time derailed in some prison where he might or might not be used as a dartboard, he'd slam the fucker, right now, drop him to the ground on this very forecourt. Then he realises his nose is dripping blood onto his suit. His dilemma? To kill or to sell, to kill or sell…

Fuck, fuck, fuck.

The young entrepreneur can't make his mind up, it's confusing.

Watching this, obscured by the petrol pumps is Carl. Carl's in a rental, it's blue and it's slow, he doesn't much like the gearbox and the fact that the indicator stalk is on the wrong side. He's had it for over a week and he's still making mistakes when turning. He's been following Joseph since he got back from Spain, following his rituals, following his routes. He's never seen an air pump used like that before, he'll give him that. Joseph's holding it like a gun now, firing little squirts into the air, with his legs further apart than they should be.

Want some more air, mother?

He's really getting into the role. The forecourt manager is banging on the window trying to get the men's attention.

He's seen suffering, his own Tamil wife never made it home. She'd been left for dead. The bunker glass is too thick for his banging to be heard. So he uses the loud speaker, it pops into life.

Pleeeas leeeav de air pumpalone.

He might as well be speaking Dutch for all the attention that got, Carl thinks.

The two rutting men don't notice, they're still deciding what to do.

The estate agent decides not to kill Joseph and screeches away. But not before placing a well aimed arching gob. It loops through the air, he's good at them, he practiced at school for years when he should have been learning, it lands, on target.

Bastard.

He shouts, looking at it hanging off Joseph's honker. Joseph wipes it off and starts to check his tyres. He isn't going to let a silly little incident like that get in the way of the job. He only gets to do one before the machine shudders and dies. He throws the nozzle back at the machine in disgust. He hates garages and the fact they don't have air machines that work or toilets in use.

Carl was hoping he had time to get some sweets, he likes to drive on them, but he hasn't got time, Joseph's getting back into his car, getting ready to drive off the forecourt. And before he knows it, he has.

Chapter 28

Et cetera, et cetera, et cetera.

Shirley says.

Luke knows what that means, he's heard that a hundred times before. Knew it before he got this new crazy education that's being thrust down his throat.

Et cetera et cetera et cetera, going on and on and on, Mum.

He repeats mockingly, he's given up with any idea of escape. Hopes that his mum will just get bored with it all and give up or have a stroke. Both would be ideal.

Now repeat this after me, *ex malo bonum.*

Shirley says it slowly, she knows it's a mouthful and tricky. He repeats it, then asks:

What does this lot mean, then?

Why does he always have to go and spoil it? Shirley thinks, why couldn't I have had a child who cared, who was interested in education and learning, like me?

It means good out of evil, Luke.

That's appropriate and what was that one yesterday, something about a conker?

He knows it's not about a conker. Shirley looks at him, he's exasperating, just like his father, in one ear, out the other. Jim's excuse had always been it was the best way for a barber to be, otherwise he'd be too bunged up, unable to take any more conversation.

Ex glande quercus, from acorn to oak. Don't you ever want to remember anything? Really, I don't know why I bother.

My thoughts exactly, Mum, why do you bother with all this? It's hardly normal.

Luke says, lifting his chained wrist as the doorbell goes. Shirley is expecting an Amazon parcel, more books, more tools for her experiment. She likes Amazon, they deliver on time, she's not so pleased about their lax tax policies though.

Before Luke can yell, the tea towel's back in. He tries to pull it out with his left hand but she stops that by slapping his face. No-one would have heard his yelling, she leaves the radio on by the front door and teaches in the loft with the hatch down, she might be a little odd but she's not a fool.

Stop it.

Luke's trying to make it as difficult as possible for her to tape him up, this could be his chance. She raises her hand again to slap him. He stops, shaking, he's defeated, broken, it was the same when he was a child, a raised hand, that's all it took. She doesn't need to slap a second time, he's like a veal calf waiting in darkness, ready to be turned into meat.

Shirley shimmies down the ladder, leaves the hatch open and looks through the spy hole, it's a man in black leather gloves, yellow topstitching all along the fingers. He's swinging a set of keys and smiling. She doesn't see a box but assumes it will be by his feet.

Shirley turns the lock, opens the door and it's Joseph. He doesn't start with a hello, how are you or a kiss, like the French and everyone else is doing now. No, he hits her full in the face, with the best he's got, uses a lot of hip and shoulder to generate power, pushes up and off his back foot, making a good if not perfect contact with his black leather knuckled glove, bought especially for the job (he'd been spending hours watching best punches ever on YouTube). Joseph had figured that YouTube could take the place of any shit teacher.

If he'd been marking it, like his old teacher had once marked him, he'd give himself at least eight out of ten, maybe more.

Miss Petticoat, Shirley, stumbles back, knocking down a wicker mirror (it came with the flat) she'd have never chosen it, she had better taste than that. She'd always meant to take it down and now it is, with her on the floor. If it had broken it might have brought her seven years of bad luck. But it survived the fall, as she has.

It hadn't been hard to enter the flat, more luck than planning on Joseph's part. The DHL driver arrived with the packet of knowledge. Joseph, sensing an opportunity, was out of his car and in front of the Romanian before he emerged from the back of his truck.

Is that for me, or my mum? Petticoat's the name.

The delivery man looked down, checked the name and handed over the parcel. His English wasn't perfect but he knew a P when he saw or heard one and knew how to save time. Before offering the parcel, he got Joseph to sign on the machine. X marks the spot, and then he added a squiggle. He wasn't stupid either.

Joseph pulls Shirley up by the hair, her lip is bleeding and her senses are fragile. He guides her to the sofa (she'd chosen it, got it at quite a good price, believed she'd charmed the salesman), it's orange with a serene magnolia scene printed all over it, tasteful, discreet.

Remember me?

Luke hears the voice as he had the punch and the mirror coming off the wall. He doesn't know if he should move, if moving would be the right option. He hadn't heard a siren and it wasn't his dad's voice but, figures someone is annoyed. He can't see the voice from his shackled position. Luke decides to stay silent, not move, not stamp and not rattle his chain. Decides it's better to let one nutter meet another. He gets the feeling that it might well be the case.

Well, what a pleasant surprise.

Joseph hits her again for old time's sake, one for the road so to speak, and one more time because he can't think of anything else to do and she's there. Her eye starts to swell, he might well have done something to her retina on the last punch, it made a good solid connection, made a crunchy sound as it hit. He makes to hit her again, throws it, but lets it come to a stop an inch from her nose. She doesn't flinch, blink or move, she can no longer see.

Remember me, Miss Petticoat? I've got some questions I wouldn't mind you answering.

He gives her a gentle slap to get some sort of eye contact going. He hadn't come with a script or a letter or a plan. He hadn't thought what he would do after he'd hit her and now he's done that he doesn't really know what to do. In fact, he's a bit bored. So he punches her again and follows that with a good connecting upper cut, he's glad he's got gloves on, his knuckles are throbbing and the yellow stitching is turning red. She falls to the floor, if he's got any questions he better start asking them because she's slipping into darkness and not going to be making any sense.

Hey teacher, leave those kids alone.

Joseph sings. He really shouldn't bother singing now, Shirley can't hear him, she's got blood trickling into her perforated ear. Joseph lets saliva drip from his mouth to her face, then does it again. He's been influenced by his encounter at the garage. He really doesn't know what else to do with her, so he starts to flick her as one would a piece of snot stuck to a finger, little flick at the eye, little flick at the ear.

Including Luke, one other person knows Joseph is in her flat and he's standing behind him now. Joseph turns and sees a leg spinning around and around in the air. Truth be told it mesmerises him, bamboozles him, a twirling leg, he'd never seen one spinning so fast. It's being swung like a lasso, generating speed and kinetic energy and Joseph finds it pleasantly hypnotic.

What the fuck...

He doesn't get to finish his question before the leg makes solid contact with his skull, it's the place where the shoe is attached that makes the most contact and hence quite a lot of damage.

Carl had followed Joseph into the building and up to Shirley. He'd already trailed him to this address, three times before.

He doesn't know who the woman is but recognises she might need hospital treatment. His army training taught him that. Pupils dilated, blood from ears, it wasn't until he saw active duty that he learnt how important knowledge was.

Luke's had a grandstand view to all the carnage once the action had moved to the front room. He couldn't believe his eyes when he saw the new arrival swinging a leg. It sure would make watching the Paralympics a different proposition for Luke now. He just hopes the man doesn't look up to the loft. If he ever does get back to the fingertip world of MyFacing he's got soooooo much to say. Twitter wouldn't have nearly enough characters to describe what's been going on.

Carl's plan is very similar to Joseph's in the fact that he doesn't really have one. Revenge is his motivator. He looks down at the man and the beaten lady next to him. The soldier scratches his lip and does the right thing, makes the 999 call. He explains the situation and that perhaps an ambulance and a police officer might be needed, does it with a Scots cross Cornish accent including all the land in between.

The woman taking the call tries to ascertain that it's not a prank, she knows for sure that there is something fishy about his accent but directs the emergency order anyway. What she really doesn't want to do is lose her job. Three useless farts in the family's enough.

Joseph has just awoken to find a leg next to his head and is patting the smooth plastic, following it up to where a body or something might be waiting. He hasn't dared open his eyes fully.

An eye for an eye and a tooth for a tooth.

Carl says, pulling his leg out of Joseph's reach, noticing the blood on his trainer, he'll have to get that cleaned. The worst thing about hitting Joseph with his leg is that it has made his balance a little tricky.

I've got something of your brother's and I want you to have it.

He scrunches up some paper and puts it in Joseph's mouth.

Now chew. Chew on fact.

Joseph does as he's told and the paper goes up and down around and around until it is swallowed.

The teacher on the floor says in a whisper.
Is that you, Lord?

She really does think she's met the merrymaker.

Chapter 29

The two officers didn't know who or what to attend to first, the woman, the man or the rattling boy. So what they did was call for back up. They weren't going to be dealing with this lot on their own. No way.

Joseph had tried to leave, he was functioning enough to know that lying next to a person who he'd nearly killed wouldn't look too clever. But he'd been tied to Miss Petticoat's ankles by a pair of her knickers, he'd tried dragging the carcass but she was too heavy. He'd given up but had got far enough to switch on the telly.

Miss Petticoat repeated something strange over and over again, which the officers tried to remember for evidence, it sounded vaguely operatic. Italian one of them thought. They should have asked Luke, he'd have told them, it was bloody Latin.

Joseph said that they'd been set upon by a Romanian gang masquerading as DHL drivers, who'd burst in on them. He told them they'd stolen all the jewellery and forced him to hit his sweet teacher until she passed out. While they laughed like the idiots they surely were. The story made Joseph cry but it didn't match up with Luke's.

As for the boy chained to the bed, he went on and on about a one legged man and that he wanted to talk to his father, but they weren't talking anymore because he'd called him a wanker. The officers didn't know what the hell was going on. That's because they weren't detectives, hadn't done the exams.

Ambulances were summoned and firefighters had come to cut the cuffs.

Swabbers and dusters arrived soon after that as the flat was taped off for forensics.

Jim had been sitting on his bike, dreaming of his good lady when he received the call. The officer didn't mention cuffs but did ask for him to come as soon as possible.

It took fifteen minutes of anxious riding to arrive at his son's side. Jim didn't need to be a genius to know something strange had been going on. He only had to look down at his white covered plastic shoes (like the ones found in local swimming pools) or his son's red, red, eyes to know that. There were men and women wearing white suits and latex gloves, dusting and daubing. The place looked like a mad fancy dress party.

You must be really ill, Son, look how many people

you've got fluffing around you?

Jim gestures with his hands, his eyes.

Yeah right, Dad.

So what's happened?

Luke looks at his dad, drops a tear and says:

Mum went psycho. Look.

And he turns his wrist over so his dad can see the marks.

Oh God, don't tell me you've become a cutter.

No, they're fucking handcuff marks.

An officer walking past hears the boy's language and tuts, thinking that's just the sort of disrespect that leads to incidents like this. Thankfully he'd never been able to sire children for himself.

Psycho? What do you mean psycho?

She locked me up in the attic, put me in cuffs and then started these Latin lessons. She went mental.

Latin? Why Latin? You sure it was Latin?

Yes, of course I'm bloody sure.

Bloody hell, the officer thinks, why does he put up with that sort of language?

Why'd she do that?

Because she's bloody mental, I don't know, you married her.

Jim was told that social services would have to get involved after such a traumatic event.

One thing about all this mess, Jim thought, was that his son's hair sure looked a lot better, just needed some tidying around the edges. He'd get to it.

Chapter 30

A week later with his trip on indefinite hold (again) unless he gets a sidecar for Luke, he's in the hospital looking at Shirley; she has white gauze over her eye, has splits and cuts. She's sleeping and looks pathetic. Jim starts looking at the minutes on the clock, wondering if to stay or not. He's already forgotten why he loved the woman on the bed or if he ever did. He's only here to ask questions. Luke won't come to see her. Jim doesn't know about all her past transgressions, her teaching methods, her strange ways and like her lying on the bed, he's very much in the dark.

The police do, they got it first from Joseph and then from others who came forward after seeing her face printed in the local paper. Some came in praise, carrying chocolate or flowers, others came carrying bile. At one stage the police even had to post a guard at the door. It's quietened down a lot now, these sort of situations normally do.

Joseph is recuperating at his parent's home with charges pending.

The doctors still don't know what it was that hit him on the head but it came with such force that they can't predict if he'll ever be quite normal again. His right eye twitches, winks, when he's talking, as if everything he's saying is a lie. They don't know if it will stop or remain ever present. It's going to make working quite hard and being taken seriously near impossible. His mother still doesn't know about the attack on the teacher or his appearances in their dead son's diary. She's just glad to have him to care for at home, something to get the Hoover going for again.

Charlie Sloane picked his son up at the hospital and spoke with the detectives and doctors. The detectives told him there'd been no Romanians and the doctors said he'd be winking for a while.

Joseph only told the partial truth to his dad about what had happened. Told him about this kung fu leg from high above that hit him and the piece of paper he'd been forced to eat.

Triad? A team of Bruce Lees? Must be, why else would they try and make me eat a fortune cookie?

Charlie didn't have an answer to that but nodded his head and took over the cooking duties that evening. He's now slowly feeding the rest of Danny's diary to his son, waters it and puts it in dishes a bit like one would if you were making papier-mâché. He's glad that his son had always been such a greedy eater and likes spice.

Charlie's got a good idea who his son's attacker might be and where the missing pages of the diary have ended up. He likes things to add up and make sense, that's his job, that's the type of man he is.

He takes satisfaction in reading the pages for the last time then putting them in his son's dishes. He's read them enough, doesn't want to read them anymore. Even if the police don't do it. Charlie's thrown the book at Joseph.

Come and visit us at
www.legendpress.co.uk

Follow us
@legend_press